A SHOCKER on SHOCK STREET

LET'S GET INVISIBLE

The HAUNTED CAR

The ABOMINABLE SNOWMAN OF PASADENA

The BLOB THAT ATE EVERYONE

IT CAME FROM OHIO: MY LIFE AS A WRITER

PLANET of the LAWN GNOMES

SON of SLAPPY

HOW I MET MY MONSTER

THE HAUNTER

DR. MANIAC WILL SEE YOU NOW

Scholastic Children's Books
An imprint of Scholastic Ltd
Euston House, 24 Eversholt Street, London, NW1 1DB, UK
Registered office: Westfield Road, Southam, Warwickshire, CV47 0RA
SCHOLASTIC, GOOSEBUMPS, GOOSEBUMPS HORRORLAND and
associated logos are trademarks and/or registered trademarks of Scholastic Inc.

First Published in the US by Scholastic Inc, 2018
First published in the UK by Scholastic Ltd, 2019

Copyright © Scholastic Inc, 2018

ISBN 978 1407 19576 6

Goosebumps books created by Parachute Press, Inc.
A CIP catalogue record for this book
is available from the British Library.
All rights reserved.

Printed by CPI Group (UK) Ltd, Croydon, CR0 4YY
Papers used by Scholastic Children's Books are made
from wood grown in sustainable forests.

Th[...] [...]es, accident[...]
and d[...] [...]ducts of the author's imagination or are u[...]d
fict[...] [...]y coincidental.

PLEASE DO NOT FEED THE WEIRDO

Goosebumps®
SlappyWorld

PLEASE DO NOT FEED THE WEIRDO

R.L. STINE

SCHOLASTIC

SLAPPY HERE, EVERYONE.

Welcome to *SlappyWorld*.

Yes, it's Slappy's world—You're only *screaming* in it! Hahaha.

Readers Beware: Don't call me a dummy, Dummy. I'm so smart, I can spell IQ forward *and* backward! Ha. I'm so bright, I use my own head as a night-light!

I'm handsome, too. I'm so good-looking, when I look in a mirror, the mirror says, "Thank you!" Hahaha.

I'm so handsome, I win an award just for waking up in the morning! Haha!

(I know that doesn't make any sense. But, hey, slave, who's going to be *brave* enough to tell me that?)

I'm generous, too. I like to share. I like to share *scary stories* to make you scream and shake all over. I don't want to give you a nightmare, slave. I want *your whole life* to be a nightmare! Hahahaha!

1

Here's a story that's a real scream. It's about a brother and sister named Jordan and Karla. They have a lot of fun at a carnival—until an ugly monster decides to have fun with *them*!

You're not afraid of ugly monsters—*are* you? Then go ahead. Start the story. I call it **Please Do Not Feed the Weirdo**.

It's just one more tale from *SlappyWorld*!

I took a big bite of the fluffy blue candy. I could feel the powdery sugar stick to my face.

Karla pointed to the cone in my hand. "Jordan, you have a spider in your cotton candy," she said.

I let out a loud "ULLLLLLP!" and the cone went flying into the air. I watched it land with a soft *plop* onto the pavement.

Karla tossed back her head and laughed. "You're too easy!"

Mom shook her head. "Karla, why are you always scaring your brother?"

She grinned. "Because it's fun?"

Grumbling to myself, I bent down and picked the cotton candy off the ground. Some of the blue stuff stuck to my sneakers. I took another bite anyway.

Some kids like to be scared and some don't. And I totally don't. I saw the Tunnel of Fear up ahead, and I knew Karla would force me to go in there with her.

My name is Jordan Keppler, and I'm twelve, a year older than Karla. I don't like to brag, but . . . I get better grades than Karla, and I'm better at sports than Karla, and I have more friends than Karla does.

So just because she likes scary things doesn't make her any kind of big deal.

I looked all around. Carnival World was crowded because it was a beautiful spring night. I saw dozens of kids on the boardwalk, going from the game booths to the rides. And I knew a lot of them were walking right *past* the Tunnel of Fear because they were like me.

What's the fun of screaming your head off, anyway?

I tossed my cotton candy cone in a trash can. "Where's that ride with the swings that go really high?" I asked.

"You mean that baby ride in the kiddie park?" Karla said.

Dad leaned over and took a big bite of Karla's cotton candy. "If you two want to go into the Tunnel of Fear, Mom and I will wait here," he said.

"No thanks," I said. "I'll wait out here, too."

Karla pressed her hands against her waist and tossed back her curly red hair. "Well, I'm not going in alone, Jerkface."

"Don't call your brother names," Mom said.

"I didn't," Karla replied. "That *is* his name." She thinks she's so smart and funny.

4

"Don't make your sister go in there alone," Dad said. He put his hands on my shoulders. "Jordan, you're not scared, are you?"

He *knew* I was scared. Why bother to ask?

"Of *course* I'm not scared," I said. "It's just that . . . I ate all that cotton candy. I have to sit down and digest it."

I know. I know. That was lame. You don't have to tell me.

Karla grabbed my hand and tugged me hard toward the entrance. "Come on, Jordan. We don't come to the carnival very often. We have to do *everything*."

I turned back to Mom and Dad. They were both making shooing motions with their hands. They were no help at all.

Don't get me wrong. I love Carnival World. I love the dart games and the corn dogs on a stick and the Ferris wheel and the Dunk-the-Clown water tank.

There are only two things I don't love. The rollercoaster rides that make you go upside down. And the Tunnel of Fear. And somehow— thanks to my sister—I knew I had both of those in my *near* future.

Karla and I walked up the wooden ramp to the tunnel entrance. "See you later!" I heard Mom shout. "If you survive!"

Ha. She and Karla have the same sick sense of humor.

5

Purple and red lights flashed all around us, and I heard deep, evil laughter—horror-movie laughter—echoing inside the tunnel. And screams. Lots of shrill screams. I couldn't tell if they were recorded or if they were from real people inside the ride.

Karla gave the young guy at the entrance two tickets, and he motioned us to the open cars. They were moving slowly along a track toward the dark cave opening where the ride began.

She pushed me into a car and slid in beside me. "This is so cool," she gushed. "We should have brought a barf bag for you."

Ha again.

"It's all fake," I said. "It's all babyish scares. Too phony to be scary. Seriously."

Wish I had been right about that.

2

As we rolled into total blackness, the door on our moving car slammed shut. A safety bar dropped down over our legs.

The car spun quickly, then slid along an invisible track beneath us. I gripped the safety bar with both hands. My eyes squinted into the darkness. I couldn't see a thing—

—Until a grinning skull shot down from above. It stopped an inch from my face, and its jagged, broken teeth snapped up and down as shrill laughter floated out.

I gasped. I didn't scream. I gripped the safety bar a little tighter.

Something damp and sticky brushed my face. I raised both hands to swipe at it, to try to push it off me.

Beside me, Karla laughed. "Yucky cobwebs," she said. She poked me. "And you know if there are cobwebs, there has to be . . ."

She didn't need to say it. At least a dozen rubbery, fat black spiders bounced over the car. I tried to brush them off my face, but there were too many of them.

The car spun again, and I stared into a wall of darkness. Were there other people in the tunnel? I couldn't see them and I couldn't hear them.

Karla screamed as a huge, caped vampire jumped into our car. *"I want to drink your bloooood!"* it exclaimed. The vampire lowered its fangs to Karla's neck—but then disappeared.

Karla shuddered. She grabbed my sleeve. "That was creepy."

"It's all computer graphics," I said. I was trying to be the brave one. But to be honest, my stomach was doing cartwheels and my throat was suddenly as dry as the cotton candy.

Then evil cackling surrounded our car, and we jolted to a stop. I rocked against the safety bar, then bounced back.

The cackling stopped.

Silence.

I heard a high-pitched scream. A girl's scream that echoed off the tunnel walls.

We sat in solid darkness. My heart started to pound.

"Think there's something wrong?" I whispered. My hands were suddenly cold and sweaty on the safety bar.

"We definitely stalled," Karla said. "Unless maybe this is all part of the ride. You know. An extra-thrill part." Typical Karla. Now she didn't sound scared at all.

My heart was pounding. "It'll probably start back up, right?"

"For sure," she said.

So we waited. Waited and listened. Listened to the heavy silence.

No voices or music or sounds from the carnival on the other side of the walls. The only thing I could hear was the throb of blood pulsing in my ears.

We waited some more.

"Cold in here," Karla murmured. "Like a tomb." She hugged herself.

"You don't think that girl's scream was a real scream—do you?" I whispered. My skin prickled.

"Why doesn't the ride start up again?" Karla whispered back, ignoring my question.

"Why are we whispering?" I asked.

Even our whispers echoed in the black tunnel.

I spread my hand over my chest. I could feel my fluttering heartbeat. I had tried to be brave. But . . . I knew I was about to lose it.

I could feel a scream forming in my throat. Feel all my muscles tighten. Feel the panic creeping up from my stomach.

How long had we been waiting in the cold, silent darkness? Ten minutes? Fifteen? More?

I gripped the safety bar so hard my hands ached. "Hey!" I shouted. "Is anyone *else* in here? Can anyone hear me? Hey!"

No answer. No one.

"I think we're the only car in here," Karla said. "Creepy, huh?"

"Can anyone hear me?" I shouted again, my voice high and shrill. "Who is in here with us? Anyone here?"

Silence.

"Hey! We need help—"

I couldn't finish my cry. Fingers wrapped around my neck from behind. Cold, bone-hard fingers . . . tightening . . . tightening. I tried to scream. But the fingers were so tight, I couldn't make a sound!

I twisted my head free and spun around in the car.

A grinning skeleton stared at me with its empty black eye sockets, an inch from my face. Its jaw squeaked up and down—and it flew up to the darkness of the ceiling.

The icy touch of its fingers still stung my skin. I was gasping for breath now.

Karla pushed my shoulder. "What is your problem? Are you having a panic attack?"

"Didn't you see that skeleton?" I cried hoarsely. "It . . . it squeezed my neck." I raised a hand and tried to rub the cold feeling away.

Karla laughed. "You idiot. That was part of the ride."

"I don't think so," I said. "Do you notice we still aren't moving? And none of the sound effects have started up again?"

"Then how would you explain it?" she demanded. "You think there's a living skeleton loose in the tunnel?"

"*Please* don't say that," I said.

She slumped back in the seat. I kept twisting around. I didn't want anyone to sneak up on me again.

"Doesn't anyone work in here?" I asked, my voice trembling.

We both waited some more. The air seemed to grow colder. I clamped my mouth shut when I realized my teeth were chattering.

After a few more minutes, Karla and I both started shouting.

"Can anyone hear us?"

"Get us *out* of here!"

"Hey—anyone?!"

"Helllllllp!"

Silence. I settled back with a long sigh.

Karla grabbed the safety bar and began to shake it. After a few tries, it popped open and slid off our legs. She started to stand up.

"What are you *doing*?" I cried.

"We have to get out of the car and walk to the exit," she said. She lowered one foot over the side.

I grabbed her and pulled her back. "No. Wait. It's . . . it's too dark."

She twisted herself free. "We can't just sit here shouting," she said. "Mom and Dad are probably worried."

"I'm worried, too," I said, my eyes darting all around. "Where's the exit? I don't see it."

"We'll use the light on our cell phones to follow

the tracks," Karla said. "You know. The tracks have to lead us out."

She lowered her feet to the ground. Then she turned and tugged my arm. "Come on, Chickenface. Follow me."

"Don't call names," I said.

"I didn't."

I stayed in the seat. I didn't want to step out of the car. I guess I felt safer sitting there. But I finally forced my legs to move and climbed down beside Karla.

She began walking along the car track. I kept glancing back, making sure nothing was sneaking up on us. It was blacker than night in the tunnel. I honestly couldn't tell if my eyes were open or closed. I put the light on from my cell phone, but it wasn't that helpful.

"Hey, wait up!" I called, my voice choked, muffled in the cold air. I squinted hard. I couldn't see Karla. "Wait up. I'm serious. You're walking too fast."

"I'm right here," she called from somewhere up ahead.

And then I stumbled. I tripped over something and fell forward.

I landed on something soft. Pain shot up my knees. I squinted into the darkness to see what I had tripped over.

"Oh nooo," I gasped.

It was a boy. A dead boy.

I scrambled to climb off him. My hand slipped on his head. His hard, wooden head.

Wait. Whoa. Not a boy. Some kind of dummy. A mannequin. Dressed in boy's clothes.

Squinting over the floor, I saw another boy mannequin. Two girl mannequins. All facedown, sprawled on the tunnel floor.

Just another scary part of the ride?

I let go of the mannequin head and pushed myself up. I'd landed hard on my right knee. I rubbed it, trying to soothe the pain away.

I stepped closer to the track and began to follow it through the darkness. I kept my eyes down. I didn't want to trip over any more mannequins.

I stopped with a gasp when I heard laughter. Cold, cruel laughter. Evil laughter in a deep woman's voice.

"Hey!" I called out. "Who's there? Is someone there?"

14

The creepy laughter echoed off the tunnel walls till it seemed to come from all directions.

"Karla? Is that you?" My voice came out high and shrill. "Karla?" Was she hiding or something? Playing a mean trick on me?

"Hey, Karla. Shout, okay? So I can find you? Karla?"

The cold woman's laughter seemed to come from right behind me. I spun around. Nothing but darkness.

"Karla? Come on. Are you trying to scare me? Stop it!" I shouted. "This isn't funny. Karla—where *are* you?"

I spun all around. I saw only a blur of black.

A loud *clank* made me jump. I heard an electric hum. Another *clank*. The cars started moving again, slowly, creaking into motion.

"Karla? Hey, Karla?" I shouted over the hum and squeak of the cars.

The woman's cold laughter rang in my ears.

I gazed around again. No Karla. No Karla.

I started toward one of the slow-moving cars. And once again, an icy hand gripped the back of my neck.

5

I gasped—and twisted my head around. And stared at Karla, who held me by the neck. "It's me, Jordan," she said. "I'm right here. What's all the shouting about?"

I jerked her hand off me. "You're not funny!" I screamed. "You did that deliberately. Why didn't you answer me? Just to scare me?"

She snickered. "Maybe."

"And why is your hand so cold?" I cried.

She shivered. "It's cold in here. Let's get out of this place." She ran to the car, grabbed the side, and leaped inside it.

I chased it along the track, pulled myself up, and slid beside her. My heart was still pounding from thinking that I'd lost her. Karla definitely has a mean streak. I honestly don't understand why she enjoys scaring me so much.

The car clattered and squeaked and led us out of the tunnel. I've never been so happy to feel the fresh air! I know I had a big grin on my face as I climbed out of the car.

I blinked hard, waiting for my eyes to adjust to the moonlight. As soon as I could focus, I scanned the carnival grounds, searching for our parents.

"Where are they?" Karla said. "They told us they'd wait for us."

"I think we came out a different door," I said. "Look. We're at the back of the Tunnel of Fear, not the front."

Two kids walked by carrying tall, soft ice cream cones. The cones were a mile high and covered in chocolate sprinkles.

Normally, I'd be drooling for one of those. But my stomach made a growling protest. My whole body was still tied in knots from our terrifying time on the ride.

I could still hear the woman's laughter from inside the tunnel. The sound sent a chill down my back. "Watch out!" a voice called. I jumped back as a man pushing a popcorn cart nearly crashed into me.

"We have to find Mom and Dad," I said. I pointed to a narrow walk at the side of the building. "We can get to the front of the Tunnel of Fear through there, I think."

We had gone only a few steps when I heard a man shouting, "Stop! Hey, you two—stop right there!"

I turned and saw a tall, long-haired man in denim overalls and a plaid lumberjack shirt running toward us. He waved something in his hand as he called to us. His dark hair bobbed behind his head as he ran. Large blue sunglasses covered most of his face.

He stopped in front of us and paused to catch his breath. He had a silver ring in one ear and a tiny silver stud in one nostril. He brushed back his long hair with one hand.

"I saw you come out of the tunnel," he said, motioning to the back of the building.

I stared at him, trying to see his eyes behind the big blue glasses. *What did he want?*

"Yeah, it was kind of messed up in there," Karla said.

"I want to apologize," he said.

"Apologize?" I asked.

He nodded. The wind tossed his hair around. "I'm Manny Ferber. I own this carnival. We had a problem with the tunnel, and I know you were kind of trapped in there."

"Kind of," I repeated. I still felt shaky and strange.

"I hope you weren't frightened," Ferber said.

"No way," I said. "It was fun."

Karla squinted at me. She mouthed the word *liar.*

Ferber brushed his hair back again. "Well, this isn't my night. The generator broke on the inflatable bouncing castle. The thing collapsed on a bunch of kids." He shook his head. "They weren't hurt. But I don't like for kids to be frightened at my carnival."

"Well, we're okay," Karla said. She was looking over Ferber's shoulder, searching for Mom and Dad, I guess.

"Here. Take these," Ferber said. He pushed a couple of long candy bars into our hands. "A little gift to make up for the trouble in the tunnel. Enjoy, okay?"

"Wow. Thanks," I said. I gazed at the candy, a giant-sized Choco-Caramel Nutty NutNut bar, one of my favorites.

Ferber gave us a salute, then turned and trotted away.

Karla raised her candy bar. "It's huge. This will last a week."

"Not with *me*," I said.

We started to head back to the path that led to the front of the tunnel. "Mom and Dad must be worried," I said. "They know we would never spend this much time in the Tunnel of Fear."

"We can explain," Karla said. She said something else, but I didn't hear her.

I was staring at a large wire cage off to the side. It was tall and wide, like a zoo cage. The shadow of the building fell over it, but I could see something was inside the cage.

"Why is that cage way back here where no one can see it?" I asked.

Karla was a few steps behind me. She hurried to catch up. "Strange," she murmured.

We strode closer. It was definitely an animal cage, with thick metal bars on all sides. Karla and I stopped in front of a large white sign hung on the front of the cage. Heavy black letters spelled out the words:

PLEASE DO NOT FEED THE WEIRDO

I stared at the sign for a moment. Then I gazed between the bars, and I saw a boy in the cage, a boy about our age. He was sitting in the middle of the cage floor, hunched on a wooden crate.

He had light brown hair and brown eyes. I couldn't see the rest of his face because he had his head propped up between his hands, his face half-buried. He leaned forward on the crate, not moving a muscle.

"Is he alive?" I whispered.

Karla squinted through the bars. "Another mannequin, I think."

No. He moved.

Karla and I stepped closer to the bars.

The boy lowered his hands to his sides and climbed off the crate. He walked over to us and raised his large, sad brown eyes.

"Please . . ." he said in a tiny voice. "Can you help me?"

"Wh-what's wrong?" I stammered. "Why are you in there?"

He shoved his hands into the pockets of his jeans. "It's kind of a long story," he said. He had dozens of freckles on his cheeks. A burst of wind ruffled his light brown hair.

"Are you locked in?" Karla asked.

The boy nodded. "Yeah. Locked in. It's ridiculous."

I glimpsed the sign again. PLEASE DO NOT FEED THE WEIRDO. *What did it mean?*

"I'm Robby Ferber," he said. "My dad owns this carnival."

"We just met him," Karla said. "See, we were stuck in the Tunnel of Fear and—"

"My dad locked me in here," Robby interrupted. "He thinks it's funny to put me in this cage with that sign." He sighed. "Big joke, huh?"

"A totally mean joke," I muttered.

Robby nodded. "Yeah. Well, he has a twisted sense of humor. He's totally unfair. He doesn't even pay me."

"Pay you?" I said.

"No. He's so cheap. He doesn't like to pay for his carnival attractions." Robby wrapped his hands around the cage bars in front of him. "I have to sit here all day like a monkey. And people walk by and stare at me."

He brushed back his hair. "I'm so bored. And mainly, I'm starving."

I suddenly realized he was staring at the big chocolate bar in my hand. I'd been so interested in his story, I forgot I was holding it.

"My dad . . . he doesn't let me eat anything until after the carnival closes," Robby said. "He's so strict. I . . . I just sit here bored out of my mind and people laugh at me because of the dumb sign."

He lowered his eyes. I thought he might start to cry.

"Do you want my candy bar?" Karla asked, raising the Nutty NutNut bar toward the cage.

I grabbed her arm. "Karla, wait." I pulled her back. I had a frightening thought. "Maybe we should listen to the sign. What if it's a real warning?" I said in a loud whisper.

"It's not a real warning," Robby said, shaking his head. "Trust me. It's my dad's stupid joke." He reached a hand through the bars.

22

"Please . . . You don't have to give me your whole candy bar. Just a few bites."

Karla and I hesitated. We stood with the big candy bars gripped in our hands.

"Please . . ." Robby repeated to Karla. "It will really help get me through the next few hours until my dad lets me out." He rubbed his belly. "Did you hear that? It's growling like crazy."

Karla leaned forward and whispered in my ear. "What do you think? Should I give it to him?"

I nodded. I glanced back at Robby. He seemed so sad and lonely. "Sure. Why not?"

Karla tore the top of the wrapper off. Then she broke off a piece of the candy and handed it to Robby through the bars.

He held it between his fingers. "Thank you," he said. "You're very generous."

"By the way," Karla said. "I'm Karla, and he's Jordan."

Robby nodded. Then he slid the chunk of candy into his mouth and began to chew it slowly. As he chewed, a smile spread over his face, the first smile we had seen from him.

He chewed a long time, then swallowed it, still smiling. "That was great," he said. "Thank you again. I *told* you that sign is just a joke." He licked his lips. "Do you think I could have just one more piece?"

"No problem," Karla said. She broke off another chunk and handed it to him.

He slid the candy into his mouth and began to chew.

"Hey!" I heard a voice shout behind us. "Hey, you kids!"

I turned and saw Robby's father, Mr. Ferber, running toward us. His long hair flew behind him, and he was wildly waving one hand in front of him. "You kids—did you feed him something?"

"Whoa!" Karla cried out as Robby grabbed the candy bar from her hand. He shoved the whole thing in his mouth, wrapper and all. He uttered a loud *gulp* as he swallowed it.

"Stop! Oh no! Oh NO!" Ferber shouted.

Robby's dark eyes bulged. He grabbed the cage bars with both hands. And then he opened his mouth wide, and a deafening noise rumbled from deep in his belly.

"URRRRRRRRRRRRP!"

The burp was so violent and disgusting, I staggered back, pulling Karla with me.

And we both watched in shock as Robby began to vomit. An ocean wave of bright orange vomit that shot up like a fountain. The vomit splashed loudly on the pavement in front of us and puddled around our shoes.

"No . . . Oh nooo . . ." I moaned. I dropped my candy bar as Robby began to transform. I grabbed on to Karla and we both backed up to the wall of the tunnel building.

Holding on to each other, we watched Robby change. Watched bright green fur sprout on his face and grow long . . . longer. The green fur quickly covered him as he grew . . . rising straight up . . . until he was at least eight feet tall.

His fur-covered paws slammed against the cage bars. He spotted my candy bar on the ground. With a deep growl, he bent and reached his green, furry arm through the bars.

He snatched the candy bar and jammed it into his mouth. I saw two rows of jagged yellow teeth as he chewed it noisily. The candy bar slid down his throat. He leaned forward and snapped his pointed teeth angrily at Karla and me. Snapped his teeth as if preparing to attack.

Then the creature tossed back his head and let out another stomach-churning "URRRR-RRRRP" from deep inside him.

He leaped up and, climbing the bars to the top, punched a hole in the cage roof with his huge fist. In seconds, he had hoisted himself out of the cage.

"No—*please!*" I cried.

He stared down at us from the top of the cage, growling, snarling at us in a rage. Then he spun around, jumped off the cage, landed hard on all fours—and raced away, growling, roaring at the top of his lungs.

"Stop him! Stop him!" Ferber chased after the creature, shaking his fists in the air. Suddenly, he turned back and narrowed his eyes at Karla and me. "What have you done?" he cried. "What have you done? Now we are DOOMED."

I heard screams throughout the park. The hard *thuds* of people running. A loud crash followed by more shrill screams.

I turned to Karla. "We have to find Mom and Dad. Make sure they're okay."

We took off, heading toward the screams. I saw people in a total panic, running in all directions. Another crash rang out. More screams.

We were nearly to the front of the Tunnel of Fear when Ferber came racing back to us. Beads of sweat glistened on his broad forehead. His eyes were wild.

"He got away! What am I going to do? What am I going to do?" he screamed, throwing his hands in the air.

We wanted to find Mom and Dad, but he blocked our path. "Couldn't you read the sign?" he demanded. "He's a dangerous monster. We were waiting for the government agents to pick him up."

"S-sorry," I stammered. "We didn't know—"

"He totally fooled us," Karla said.

Ferber swept his long hair out of his eyes. "Yes, he's good at that. Now he'll be impossible to catch."

"Why won't the police be able to track him down?" Karla asked.

"Because he's like a chameleon," Ferber said. "He can change. He can make himself look like *anyone.*"

The screams had died down. An eerie silence fell over the park. Robby had escaped, and it was all our fault.

I heard sirens in the distance. Someone must have called the police. Too late.

All our fault. All our fault.

"If he was so dangerous, why did you keep him in that cage?" Karla demanded.

Ferber shook his head. "I—I had him locked up inside. But he escaped this morning. I finally chased him into this cage. I thought I could leave him there until the federal agents came."

He sighed. "It . . . was a big mistake."

The police sirens grew louder. I could see red and blue flashing lights from the front of the park.

Ferber tossed up his hands again in a helpless gesture. Then, without another word, he ran to meet the police.

I turned and saw Mom and Dad hurrying

toward us. "Are you okay?" they both shouted at once.

They wrapped us in hugs. "We were so worried," Mom said, her voice trembling. "We didn't know where you were."

"People were yelling and screaming and running for their lives," Dad said. "We didn't know why. We were in a total panic."

I didn't want to upset them. I didn't want to tell them that Karla and I were the ones who let a terrifying creature loose.

"We came out the back of the tunnel, and we couldn't find you," I said. "Can we go?" I asked.

Mom and Dad didn't argue about it. "The park is almost empty," Mom said. "Everyone was desperate to get away."

Dad shook his head. "I've never seen so many crying kids. They were all just terrified."

"What could have happened to scare everyone?" Mom asked.

Karla and I didn't answer.

"I guess we'll hear about it on the news," Dad said.

The four of us started to walk toward the exit. I saw four or five black-and-white police cars parked right on the carnival grounds. Dark-uniformed officers had spread out and were moving in twos through the booths and rides.

They were searching slowly and carefully. But I didn't think they'd find Robby. He was probably miles away already.

Karla moved close and whispered in my ear. "Don't you want to tell Mom and Dad what really happened?"

I shook my head. "Not now. I don't want to think about it. Let's just get away from here."

"How was the Tunnel of Fear?" Dad asked as we pushed through the turnstiles at the exit. "Jordan, were you brave in there?"

"It totally sucked," I said. "It all broke down, and we were stuck in the dark. And no one came to help us."

"That's why we were gone for so long," Karla said.

Mom tsk-tsked. "Talk about a bad day. This was crazy! A total horror show."

You don't know the half of it, I thought.

I pictured Robby roaring through the woods. Ripping trees out of the ground. Grabbing birds and squirrels and shoving them into his mouth.

I climbed into the backseat of the car beside Karla. What was that sour smell? It took me a while to realize it was the stink of Robby's vomit on my shoes. I slid the car window open and took deep breaths.

"Jordan, are you okay?" Mom asked from the front seat. "You look very pale."

"I'm fine," I lied. "Just a little carsick, I guess."

"Carsick?" Dad cried. "Jordan, we're still in the parking lot!"

Okay. Okay. That was lame. Best I could do at the moment.

Dad backed the car out of the parking space. I saw a long line of cars heading to the exit. People were desperate to get away. Two kids were rubbing their eyes and crying in the backseat of the car ahead of us.

The moon was shining behind the trees, and the sky had turned gray. We all got quiet. Dad turned on his favorite Motown music, and he and Mom sang along with it the rest of the way home.

Was I happy to get home? Three guesses.

Mom and Dad headed to the kitchen. "You kids didn't eat much at the carnival," Mom said. "Your father and I are going grocery shopping. Want to come?"

"Not me," I said quickly.

"Okay, I'll come," Karla said. "If I can buy Double Stuf Oreos." She has a thing about Double Stuf Oreos. I told her I read online that they don't really have double the cream filling. But Karla doesn't care.

I started down the hall to my room.

"Back in a flash," Dad called. I heard the kitchen door slam behind them.

My room is at the end of the hall, past a bathroom and Karla's room. My door was closed. I didn't remember closing it.

I turned the knob, pushed the door open—and gasped. "What are *you* doing here?" I cried.

Robby sat in my desk chair, the glow of my laptop screen on his face. His boy face. He stood up as I took a step into the room. "Hi," he said. He had a strange, shy smile on his face. Like he was embarrassed.

I stayed in the doorway. I didn't want to get too close.

"How . . . How did you get here?" I stammered.

He shrugged. "I followed you home." The shy smile remained on his face. "I like your room, Jordan."

I didn't know what to say. I was terrified, yes. But I was also curious.

I mean, there he was, a human-looking, brown-haired boy with freckles on his cheeks. He wore the same flannel shirt and straight-legged jeans as when he was in the cage.

Outside my bedroom window, a cloud drifted across the moon. The window was open, and a chilly breeze blew into the room. I shivered. And crossed my arms in front of me.

"You have to go," I said. "You can't stay here. You're a monster."

"No, I'm not," he said, shaking his head. "I'm not a monster. I'm just a kid with a small problem."

Was that a joke?

I had a sudden urge to call out to Mom and Dad for help. But then I remembered they had gone grocery shopping. I was alone. Alone in the house with a monster.

He climbed off my desk chair and took a few steps toward me.

A warning chill shot down my back. My muscles stiffened. I prepared to run.

"Don't look so frightened," he said softly. "I won't hurt you."

"No. I—" I didn't know what to say. I just kept thinking, *How can I get rid of him?*

"I came to apologize," he said. "For tricking you and your sister."

I swallowed. "Apologize?"

He nodded. "I'm really sorry for vomiting all over you. And for scaring you. That was terrible."

I nodded. "It was kind of surprising."

He shuffled his feet. His head was lowered. "I don't know what came over me, Jordan. I really don't. That's why I came to apologize."

"Okay," I said. He was acting so normal, shy and quiet. He really seemed sincere. "Do you . . . uh . . . plan to go back to the carnival?"

He squinted hard at me. "Go back? I don't think so."

"Well . . ." I hesitated. I didn't want to get him angry. "What do you plan to do?"

He shrugged. "Hard to say. I've got to think about it. You know. Make a plan."

He took another step toward me. I backed into the doorway, ready to run down the hall.

"Ferber isn't really your father, *is* he?" I said.

He didn't answer. Just kept squinting at me. A wave of brown hair fell over his face, but he made no attempt to push it back.

The silence in the air suddenly felt heavy. Menacing.

Finally, he spoke. "I'm really hungry," he said. He rubbed the front of his flannel shirt. "My stomach feels . . . empty. You know that feeling?"

"Sure," I said. "But I can't—"

"You know that feeling when you're so hungry, your stomach actually hurts?"

I nodded. "Yeah."

"Maybe you could bring me some food, Jordan." His eyes became big and pleading. He rubbed his stomach again.

"I . . . I don't think so," I said. "I'm all alone here and—"

"If you bring me some food, I'll go away." He raised his right hand. "I swear."

I studied him, my mind spinning. "It's not a good idea," I said. "I'm sorry, Robby, but I don't think I can trust you."

He kept his right hand raised. "No. Seriously, I swear," he said. "Give me a little food, and I promise. I'll go away and never bother you again."

I was tempted. Was he telling the truth?

"I'm not a bad guy," Robby said. "You shouldn't judge me by what happened at the carnival. That was so freaky. It even creeped *me* out. But it won't happen again. No way."

I took another few seconds to make up my mind. "Okay," I said. "Let's go to the kitchen. We'll see what's in the fridge."

10

I led the way down the hall to the kitchen. Robby walked slowly, peering into each room we passed. He stopped in the doorway to Karla's room and studied it.

"Nice house," he said quietly. "Everything is so clean."

"Where do *you* come from?" I asked.

"I don't know."

Weird answer.

I motioned to the tall stools at the kitchen counter. "Take a seat," I said. "I'll see what's in the—"

My eyes stopped at a box on the counter beside the fridge. Honey Nut Cheerios. "Robby, do you like cereal?"

"Yeah. Sure." He was perched on the tall stool at the end. He leaned over the counter and twirled the salt and pepper shakers in his hands. "This is really nice of you, Jordan. You're a good friend."

"Okay," I said. I didn't know what else to say to that. "But you'll keep your promise—yes?"

He nodded solemnly and raised his right hand again.

I poured the cereal into a bowl. Then I added milk and carried the bowl and the cereal box to Robby at the counter.

"Thank you," he said quietly. He picked up the spoon, slid it around in the Cheerios, and then took a bite. "Mmmmm," he said, chewing. "This is awesome, Jordan."

I stood beside the counter watching him eat the cereal. He looked like any kid my age sitting on a stool, eating a bowl of cereal. He dipped the spoon into the bowl slowly, carefully. He had a smile on his face as he downed each spoonful.

I let out a long whoosh of air. I could feel myself starting to relax a little. Watching him eat, I thought about Mr. Ferber.

Should I try to call him as soon as Robby leaves? Should I tell him Robby was here? Or should I let Robby enjoy his freedom?

"I could make you a peanut butter sandwich," I said. "Would that be good?"

He nodded. "Good." He had milk running down his chin.

I bent down to the bread drawer and lifted out a loaf of bread. I stood up and started to reach for the peanut butter jar. But I stopped when I saw Robby pick up the Cheerios box.

39

He raised it above his head, tilted it to his face—and let the Cheerios come sliding out, into his open mouth.

"Hey, uh . . . Robby?" I said.

An avalanche of Cheerios poured down his throat. Lots of them missed his mouth and sprayed onto the kitchen floor, bouncing all over.

"Robby, you're spilling—" I started.

I gasped when he ripped the box in two and shoved one half into his mouth. His eyes were wild now as he frantically chewed the cardboard. He swallowed the half with a loud *gulp*. Then he shoved the other half of the box into his mouth.

"Stop it!" I cried. "Robby—you promised!"

He jumped off the stool and lurched toward the counter.

"Hey—" I cried out as he pushed me out of the way. I stumbled sideways and hit the breakfast table.

I turned to see Robby shoving fistfuls of bread into his mouth. He made loud gurgling and slurping noises as the gobs of bread slid down his throat.

When the bread was all eaten, he tossed the wrapper on the floor. Then he turned to me, his eyes bulging, his face bright red. And a loud, stomach-wrenching "URRRRRRRRRP!" erupted from deep inside him.

"No. Please . . . Please . . ." I begged.

He made a few gagging sounds. Then a stream of bright orange vomit spewed from his mouth. It splashed onto the kitchen counter and sprayed the floor.

He exploded in another deafening "URRR-RRRP." He sprayed orange vomit over the front of the fridge and across the stove top.

And as he choked and spewed, his body changed again. And he expanded into the ugly, green fur-covered creature Karla and I had seen at the carnival.

"No—please!" I shouted. I raised my hands in front of me as a wave of vomit shot toward me.

He began to roar—like an angry bear—and swing his arms crazily from side to side. With a terrifying growl, he ripped a cabinet door off its hinges and tossed it down the hall.

I ducked and covered my head as another cabinet door went flying. When I raised my eyes, I gasped in shock. Mom and Dad walked in through the kitchen door with Karla close behind.

"Jordan! What have you DONE?" Mom shrieked.

"It wasn't me!" I cried. "It wasn't me. It was HIM!"

I turned and pointed to the monster.

But there was no one there.

11

Dad groaned. "Ohhh. What's that smell?" He pinched his fingers over his nose.

"It . . . it's vomit," I stammered.

"Jordan—you're *sick*?" Mom cried.

"I *told* you—it wasn't me!" I exclaimed.

They still hadn't moved from the doorway. Karla pushed between them and stepped into the kitchen. She set down the grocery bag she had been carrying.

"Listen to him, Mom. He's telling the truth," Karla said.

"But—but—but—" Dad sputtered like a motorboat starting up.

"It was the monster that escaped from the carnival," I said.

Mom gasped. "A monster? Is *that* what made everyone panic?"

"His name is Robby," I said. "He looks like a normal boy, but when you feed him he turns into a monster . . ."

"A real monster?" Mom cried. "In my kitchen? A monster who throws up orange gunk everywhere and rips the cabinets apart?"

Dad slapped his forehead. "Why didn't you tell us you saw a monster?"

Mom's mouth hung open. "That's why the people in the park were screaming," she said. "A monster. A real monster."

"Why didn't you tell us?" Dad asked again.

"We . . . we didn't want to worry you," Karla said.

"We . . . never thought we'd see him again," I said. "But . . ."

Karla pointed to the floor. "Look. Orange paw prints. Look at them. He must have stepped in his own vomit."

We walked behind her as she followed the trail of footprints on the floor. The front door stood wide open. The footprints led right out the door.

"Maybe he's still in the neighborhood," I said. I peered out to the street. "Maybe he's still nearby."

"Quick. Call the police," Mom said. "Call 911."

"Are you crazy?" Dad cried. "What are you going to tell the police? That a boy turned into a monster and got sick in our kitchen? Do you honestly think *anyone* would believe that story?"

"I know *someone* who would believe it," I said.

"So do I," Karla said. "Mr. Ferber. The guy who owns the carnival."

"We have to tell him," I insisted. "We have to tell him that his monster is in our neighborhood. That he was *here*."

"Unbelievable," Dad murmured, his eyes on the footprints on the floor. "Unbelievable."

Mom had tears in her eyes. She kept biting her lips, blinking hard. She covered her face with both hands. "You could have been hurt. You were all alone here with a . . . with a monster!"

Dad put a hand on her shoulder. "Jordan is fine. It's okay. But there's a monster on the loose. We have to find that carnival owner."

And that's what we did. Mom and Dad put the groceries away. They opened all the windows in the house to try to let the smell out.

Then the four of us piled into the car and made the long drive back to Carnival World. It was now chilly with storm clouds low overhead, threatening rain. Gusts of wind blew our little Prius from side to side on the highway.

Dad leaned over the steering wheel, peering straight ahead into the passing darkness, gripping the wheel tightly with both hands. "Nasty night," he muttered.

We didn't talk much. I could see Mom shaking her head in the front seat.

Karla moved close to me in the backseat. She swept back her coppery hair and whispered in my ear. "We should have called the police. What can that guy Ferber do?"

"Maybe he knows a way to capture him," I whispered back. "I mean, he captured Robby in the first place, didn't he?"

"Do you think Robby is still in our neighborhood?" she whispered. "I'll bet he took off as soon as he trashed our kitchen. He's probably miles away."

"Hope so," I said. I kept picturing him growing furry, growing huge, turning from a quiet, normal boy into an ugly, roaring beast. Would I ever be able to get that picture from my mind?

Our tires crunched over the gravel as Dad pulled the car into the Carnival World parking lot. The lot was empty. Up ahead, I could see that everything was dark, closed for the night. A single light burned dimly over the entrance.

"Whoa." A gust of wind blew my hair straight up as I climbed out of the car.

Karla laughed. "You look like a terrified cartoon character!"

"Thanks a bunch," I muttered. I pushed my hair down with both hands.

The wind swirled through the carnival grounds. Beyond the gate, I saw that most of the rides had been covered in canvas tarps. The tarps shivered and bumped in the gusting winds. The game booths were all dark and shuttered.

We stepped through the turnstiles. No one in sight. A few dim lights dotted the area. Huddled close together, the four of us began to walk slowly down the main aisle.

"What makes you think this guy Ferber stays at his carnival after it's closed?" Mom asked Dad.

Dad shrugged. "I didn't really think about it," he said. "I didn't know where else to look for him."

"Yeah. Maybe he has a little house or a trailer in the back," I said.

"Or maybe this is a wild goose chase," Mom murmured. She shivered. Dad put an arm around her shoulders.

A shrill screech made me gasp. Karla grabbed my arm.

A creature darted out from the side of a game booth. A scrawny black cat, its head down, tail up stiff behind it, running hard.

I squinted into the dim yellow light and saw what it was chasing. A large rat. The rat crossed the aisle and swung behind an ice cream booth, with the cat close behind.

My heart was pounding in my chest. "I don't like rats," I muttered.

Karla let go of my arm. She laughed. "The carnival isn't so great after dark," she said.

"We'll walk to the end of this aisle," Dad said. "If we don't find Mr. Ferber, we'll give up and go home."

We heard a sharp squeal. I knew what it was, but I didn't want to think about it. It was the sound the rat made as it was caught by the cat.

"I'm surprised Mr. Ferber doesn't have a security guard," Mom said.

"Maybe he has security cameras," Dad replied.

We walked a little farther. I stopped when I heard a voice. A woman's voice, muffled by the whoosh of the wind. "Listen," I said.

Everyone stopped. The wind died down for a moment, and we could hear the woman's laughter clearly. Cold, cruel laughter, repeating itself endlessly.

"Where *is* she?" Mom said. "Why is she laughing like that?"

I pointed. "It's from the Tunnel of Fear," I said. "Someone must have forgotten to turn it off."

The Tunnel of Fear stood in front of us. Its entrance doors were shut, and the cars stood still on their track, gleaming dully under a single light on the building roof.

I shuddered, thinking about the frightening time Karla and I had spent in there. And as I thought about it, something moved in the darkness behind the tunnel building. A dark shadow against the gray shadows, moving fast.

"Whoa." I uttered a cry as the figure moved closer. It took me a few seconds to realize it was

Mr. Ferber. He was running fast, waving both arms at us.

"Get out!" he shouted. His long hair flew behind him as he ran, his long legs taking big strides, boots thudding the pavement. "Get out! You are trespassing!"

He stopped a few feet ahead of us, eyes wide with anger. Dad stepped forward, as if to protect us. Ferber swept his hair back off his face. His eyes went from Dad to Mom and then stopped on Karla and me.

"I recognize you," he said. "What are you doing here? Did you lose something?"

"No," I answered. "We saw the monster. He was at our house."

Ferber blinked. "The monster? You mean Robby? The boy from the cage?"

"Yes, of course," I said.

"How many monsters do you *have*?" Dad chimed in.

Ferber ignored him. He kept his eyes on me. "He was at your house? You mean he followed you home?"

I nodded. "He followed us home. I . . . I made a mistake. I gave him food again. He trashed our kitchen and then—"

"We came to find you right away," Karla said. "He might still be in our neighborhood. He—"

"No, he isn't," Ferber interrupted.

I stared at him. "What do you mean?"

"He isn't in your neighborhood," Ferber replied. "Because I captured him."

I uttered a startled gasp. "Captured him? You mean you have him back?"

Ferber nodded. "I got him. No problem. He hardly put up a fight."

He grinned and pointed to a building behind the Tunnel of Fear. "I have him locked up inside. Safe and sound. He won't be escaping again."

"That's great news," Dad said. He sighed and turned to us. "I guess we made this trip for nothing."

"You did the right thing," Ferber told him. "You would have been very helpful if I hadn't already acted."

"Well, good night," Dad said.

"Glad there's a happy ending to this story," Mom added.

Ferber nodded. "Sorry for your trouble. Come back to Carnival World anytime, okay? Free admission—for life. I mean it."

"Wow, thanks!" Karla said. "We can come back every week?"

Ferber laughed. "Sure. Every week."

"Forget it," I murmured to her. "I'm not going back in the Tunnel of Fear. I know that's what you were thinking."

"Stop reading my mind," Karla shot back.

The ride back home was a happy one. Dad played his Motown music and we all sang along.

Even Mom, although I knew she was thinking about the horrible kitchen cleanup still to be done.

As we pulled up the driveway, Dad patted her arm. "I'm going to hire a professional cleaning service tomorrow for the kitchen," he said. "I don't want you to touch anything."

"But . . . but how will we explain the gallons of orange vomit?" Mom sputtered.

Dad grinned. "We'll tell them Jordan drank too much tomato juice."

That was Dad's idea of a joke. Karla was the only one who laughed. But of course she would.

I headed straight for my room. What a long day! The smell in the house was pretty gross. I closed my bedroom door and it was a little better.

Yawning, I changed into my pajamas, turned out the light, and climbed into bed. The window was closed.

The wind outside was still gusting. It made the window glass rattle. Gazing out the window from my bed, I could see the pale half-moon high in the sky.

I yawned again. I started to fade into sleep. But a knock on my door startled me, and I sat up, instantly alert.

The door swung open and Karla came striding into the room in her long nightshirt. "Are you asleep?"

"Well . . . not anymore," I said.

Is that the stupidest question you can ask someone—*Are you asleep?* There can only be one answer.

"I'm totally wired," she said, dropping down on the edge of my bed. "I'll never get to sleep."

"You have to keep trying," I said. "You'll be surprised. After a while, you will—"

I stopped talking when I heard a loud tap on the bedroom window. I felt my heart skip a beat. *Was it the wind?*

Karla jumped to her feet. She heard it, too.

Another *tap-tap* on the window glass. Louder this time.

We both crossed the room to the window. And we both let out cries as we stared at Robby, lit by the pale moon, peering in at us, his knuckles raised to the glass.

Tap tap.

12

"Don't open the window," I said, taking a step back. "He's dangerous."

Robby moved forward and pressed his face against the glass. The moonlight made his brown hair glow. He gazed in at us with pleading eyes and tapped on the window again.

"He's pretending to be sad," Karla said. "But he can't fool us again." She reached for the window handles.

"What are you doing?" I cried.

"I'm going to open the window and tell him he has to go away."

I shook my head. "Please—don't. You saw what he did to the kitchen."

"I won't let him in," Karla said. "We'll be very careful, okay?"

I knew she was showing off. Showing how much braver she was than me.

"I don't get it," I said. "Ferber said he captured Robby. He said he had him safe and sound."

Karla slid the window up. She glared out at Robby. "What are you doing here?" she demanded.

"I just want to talk," he said. "Can I come in?"

He didn't wait for an answer. He grabbed the windowsill with both hands and hoisted himself into the room. He shivered and brushed himself off.

The wind blew the curtains into the room. Karla pushed the window shut. She and I stared at Robby with our arms crossed in front of us.

"How did you get out again?" I asked. "Ferber said he captured you. He said he had you locked away."

A faint smile crossed Robby's face. "No, he didn't," he said.

"He told us he captured you without a fight," Karla said.

"No, he didn't," Robby repeated.

"We talked to him," I said. "We—"

"No, Jordan, you didn't talk to him," Robby said. He crossed the room and lowered himself onto my desk chair. "You didn't talk to Ferber at the carnival. That was *me*."

My mouth dropped open. "You mean—?"

"I have this weird ability," he said. "I can make myself look like other people." He smiled again. "It comes in handy sometimes."

"I don't believe it," Karla said, shaking her head. "I don't believe that was you—"

"Why would Ferber stay at the carnival after closing?" Robby asked. "He has an apartment in the next town. You were talking to me the whole time."

Karla dropped back onto the edge of my bed. I stood there, my arms still crossed tightly, as if protecting myself. "Well, okay. You fooled us. But what are you doing here? What do you want?"

"I came back to apologize," he said, lowering his eyes. "I . . . I'm really sorry for what I did."

I uttered a disgusted groan. "Robby, you always apologize. But—"

"I know. I know," he said. "I admit it, Jordan. I have a problem."

"A *problem*?" I cried.

"It's something I have to deal with, okay? But I wanted to come back and tell you how sorry I am about everything. And I want to help clean up the mess I made."

Karla and I exchanged glances. Was he *serious*?

"I'm ready to start cleaning," Robby said, rolling up the sleeves of his flannel shirt. "I mean it."

"Right now?" Karla said. "We can't clean the kitchen now, Robby. Our parents are asleep."

"I'll come back tomorrow," Robby said. "I've caused you a lot of trouble, and I want to make up for it."

We both stared at him, unable to think of what to say.

"I'm a good guy," he said. "No kidding. I never mean to hurt anyone."

I moved to the window and started to slide it open. "I think you have to go now," I said.

He nodded. "Okay. Thanks for letting me come in and apologize."

"No problem," I said.

He stopped halfway to the window. "I want to ask you one more thing. It's kind of embarrassing. But . . . do you think you could bring me some food before I go? I'm just a little bit hungry."

13

My mouth dropped open. "No way," I said.

Robby pushed his hands together in front of him, as if he were begging. "Please. Not anything big. Just a little snack, and I'll go away. I promise. You'll never see me again."

I saw Karla get ready to protest. But I answered quickly. "Okay. Stay right here, Robby. I'll go to the kitchen and bring you a snack."

He grinned at me. "Thanks, Jordan. You're a friend. And I swear I'll keep my promise."

I turned and walked into the hall. I wasn't surprised when Karla came running after me.

She grabbed me by the shoulders and spun me around. "Are you *crazy*? What are you doing? Are you really going to bring him food?"

I raised a finger to my lips. "Ssshhhh. No way," I whispered. "I'm not going to bring Robby food. I'm going to wake up Dad. Dad can grab him and hold him, and we can call the police."

Karla nodded. "Okay. I get it. Hurry."

My parents' room was on the other side of the kitchen. I held my nose as I crossed the kitchen floor. The odor was totally gross. I couldn't see well in the dark, and I felt my bare feet step in sticky puddles. *Yuck.*

The door to my parents' bedroom was open. I burst in, whispering, "Dad, Dad—wake up!"

He's a light sleeper. He sat up instantly, blinking at me in the darkness. "Jordan? What's wrong?"

"Hurry, Dad," I said. "Robby. The monster. He's in my room. You can grab him."

Dad climbed out of bed. His hair was wild about his face. He adjusted his pajama pants. "He's here?"

I nodded. "Hurry. I promised him food. You can hold him. I'll call 911."

Dad followed me through the kitchen and into the hall. Our bare feet thudded against the wooden floorboards.

Light seeped from my room into the dark hall. Dad and I burst into the room together. "There he is!" I cried.

Dad swept his gaze all around. "Where?"

Karla was hunched on the side of my bed, looking glum. "He's gone," she said. "He said he knew it was a trick."

Dad ran to the open window and stuck his

head out. "I don't see him," he said. "He must have run."

I shook my head. "We almost had him. We were so close."

Karla sighed and stared out the window. "Think he'll be back?"

SLAPPY HERE, EVERYONE.

Think he'll be back? Of *course* he'll be back.

How *lame* would this story be if Robby ran off and they never saw him again?

Jordan and Karla would be stuck there staring at each other, and what kind of story is that? *Borr-ring!*

Know what I think? I don't think Robby went very far. Know why? He doesn't like to miss a meal!

Hahahaha!

All this talk is making me *hungry*. Know what's keeping me from gulping down a few cheeseburgers, a basket of fries, and a tall, thick shake?

I don't have a stomach!

Hahahaha!

Now let's see what happens in school the next day . . .

14

The next morning, Mom wanted to walk us to school, but she said she couldn't. "I have a doctor appointment at eight," she said.

"Don't worry. It's only four blocks," I said.

Mom frowned. "But there might be a monster out there," she said.

She thought about it for a moment. "Why don't you call your friend Bernardo across the street? You can walk with him if it will make you feel safer."

"No good," I said. "Bernardo is always late. It's crazy in his house. He's never ready on time."

"I think we'll be okay for four blocks," Karla said. "And I have my phone. I can always call you if there's trouble."

So, Karla and I walked to school. And I don't think I was ever more tense or more alert. I mean, I saw every blade of grass and every leaf on every tree. I saw who was riding in every car

60

that passed and watched every kid who rode past us on a bike.

I suddenly had super-eyes. I could see squirrels in high tree limbs and I could count the feathers on robins picking at worms in the grass.

Well, maybe I'm exaggerating a little. But believe me, I was on guard and at attention, ready for anything. Because I knew Robby had to be around. I knew for sure that he wasn't finished with us.

And sure enough, Karla and I had walked only one block when I heard a shout, turned, and saw someone running across the street, coming at us.

"Kids, wait up!" he called.

I'd been waiting for this, but it startled me anyway. I bumped into Karla, and we both nearly fell to the sidewalk.

"Hey, there you are," he said. It was Mr. Ferber. His long hair was tied back in a ponytail. He wore an oversized red-and-blue *Carnival World* T-shirt over denim jeans.

"Have you seen Robby?" he asked. "We have to capture him. He's very dangerous."

Karla and I stared back at him without answering. Finally, Karla broke the silence. "We know it's you, Robby. We know you're not Ferber."

"You can't fool us a second time," I said.

He rolled his eyes. "What are you talking about? Of *course* I'm Ferber."

"No, you're not," Karla insisted. "Give it up."

"You fooled us at the carnival last night. You're not going to fool us again."

His eyes went wide. "At the carnival? You were there last night?"

"Give us a break," I said. I turned and started walking toward school. "We're not stupid."

"But . . . but . . ." he sputtered. "Hey, wait up." He chased after us. "I'm Ferber. For real. I'm not Robby."

Karla turned to face him again. "If you're Ferber, how did you find us? How did you know where to look for us?"

"Your father paid for the carnival tickets with a credit card," he replied. "I tracked down your address from the card."

I studied his eyes. He seemed to be telling the truth.

"Listen, has Robby been here?" he demanded. "Have you seen him? You haven't fed him— have you?"

Karla shook her head. "Sorry. I still don't believe you're Ferber. You have to prove it."

He frowned at her. "How am I supposed to do that? Do you want to see my driver's license?"

"No," she said. "That won't prove anything."

He thought for a moment. "Okay," he said. "I can prove I'm not Robby. No problem."

"How?" I said.

"Give me something to eat," he said. He pointed at Karla's backpack. "What have you got in there? Give me some food and I'll prove I'm not Robby."

We both stared at him.

A shiver of fear rolled down my back. "It's a trick," I murmured. "Don't give him anything."

He raised his right hand. "I swear. Give me something to eat, and you'll see I'm Ferber, not Robby." He glanced all around. "Hurry. We're wasting time. Robby may be getting away."

Karla and I exchanged glances. She swung her backpack off her shoulders and began to search inside it. "Here," she said finally. She pulled out a banana and held it out to Ferber.

He rolled his eyes. "About time." He grabbed the banana, peeled it, and shoved it chunk by chunk into his mouth.

Karla and I stood there watching him carefully as he swallowed the last bite. My whole body tensed. I knew what was about to happen.

He wiped his mouth with the back of his hand and handed the banana peel back to Karla. "Okay. I ate it," he said. "Now do you believe me?"

"Let's wait a minute or two," Karla answered.

15

We had a long staring match. Karla and I took a few steps back until we were standing at the curb.

I readied my arms to shield me if the vomit began to spew.

But no. Nothing happened. We stood there just looking at one another.

"Satisfied?" Ferber said finally. "Now do you believe I'm not Robby disguised as Ferber?"

"Guess so," I said. "But last night . . ."

"He must have followed you home because you were the ones who let him out of his cage," Ferber said. "Now he thinks he belongs to you."

I rolled my eyes. "Oh, fantastic," I said sarcastically.

"He's probably nearby," Ferber said, his eyes darting all around, checking out the lawns and houses. "Maybe he thinks you're his protectors. But . . . we have to round him up as soon as possible. Before he does a lot of damage. Before he *hurts* people."

"Jordan made a mistake last night," Karla told him. "He fed Robby. Now our kitchen is destroyed."

Ferber tsk-tsked. "Don't ever feed him. He only gets dangerous after you feed him."

I saw some kids across the street running along the sidewalk. "Karla, we're going to be late," I said. "We have to go."

Ferber reached into his jeans pocket and pulled out two cards. "Here. Take these. It's my card. See my phone number? Call me fast if you see him. I'll be waiting."

He turned and trotted away. I tucked the card into my jeans pocket. Karla and I crossed the street.

We had walked only a few steps on the next block when I heard a shout. I turned and saw someone else running across the street, waving both hands in the air.

"Hey—wait up, guys!"

It was my friend Bernardo. He ran up to us, breathing hard. Bernardo is a big kid, tall and wide, with a big belly that bounces in front of him.

He looked kind of messed up. His straight black hair was unbrushed and one side stood straight out. And his blue shirt wasn't buttoned right, so that one side hung down over the other.

But that's Bernardo. He would never win an award for neatness.

"Hey, guys," he said. He put a sweaty hand on my shoulder. "What's up?"

"We're going to be late," I said. "The first bell is in five minutes."

"So what else is new?" he said. He lowered his eyes to my backpack. "Guess what, dude? My dad was busy with the twins, and he forgot to give me breakfast again. Do you have something I could have? Like a bag of chips or something?"

He put his hands together like he was begging. "Please. Please. Do you have like an apple or maybe a muffin? What have you got? A couple of cookies? A Fruit Roll-Up? I didn't have any breakfast. C'mon—what have you got?"

16

I snickered. Bernardo seemed so desperate. The poor guy. The new twins got all the attention at his house, and he was pretty much left to take care of himself.

Which he wasn't too good at.

I swung my backpack around. I knew Dad had put a bag of tortilla chips in my lunch. "Hold on, Bernardo," I said as I fumbled in the bag.

Karla grabbed my arm. "No. Jordan—don't give it to him!" she cried.

Bernardo rolled his eyes. "Karla, what's your problem? You guys always share your lunches with me. Right?"

"Today is different," Karla said, her eyes on me, warning me. "It's nothing personal, Bernardo. It's just—"

"He's okay," I interrupted her. "Look at him. No one could imitate that."

"Don't do it, Jordan," Karla said again, tightening her grip on my arm.

"He's okay," I repeated. "This can't be Robby. Robby wouldn't know about Bernardo's twin sisters. And he wouldn't know that Bernardo asks for food all the time."

Karla let out an exasperated sigh. "I'm warning you . . ."

I handed Bernardo the bag of tortilla chips.

He ripped off the top, tilted the bag over his mouth, and dumped all the chips into his mouth at once. His cheeks puffed out wide as he chewed and chomped, noisily, juicily.

He chewed for a long time. Then he swallowed the huge glob of chewed-up chips with a loud *gullllp*.

He grinned at us. "Thanks, guys. That was a great breakfast."

I opened my mouth to say something—then stopped. And Karla and I both cried out in horror as he began to *erupt*.

17

"ROARRRRRRPP."

The explosion from Bernardo's belly sent Karla and me stumbling back.

My heart skipped a beat and I froze, waiting for the fur to sprout all over his body, watching for him to rise up, roaring and thrashing.

But no. He grinned and rubbed his belly.

It was just a burp. Typical Bernardo.

I burst out laughing. Karla looked pale. Her whole body shuddered.

"Thanks, guys," Bernardo said again. "Come on. We're going to be late."

The three of us began to trot. My legs felt shaky. Karla dragged me aside. "That was *terrifying*," she whispered.

I laughed again. "Bernardo is *always* terrifying."

She poked me hard with her elbow. "You know what I mean. He could have been Robby. We

69

know Robby can make himself look like *anyone*."

I shifted the backpack on my shoulders. "What can we do? We can't be scared of *everyone*."

"We'll just have to be careful," Karla said. She sighed. "Maybe we'll get lucky. Maybe Robby decided to go somewhere else. Maybe he's far away by now."

"Yeah. Maybe," I said. But I didn't believe it.

"Hey, guys, what's your problem?" Bernardo called from the corner. "Hurry up!"

"No problem," I called. And we ran the rest of the way to school.

I was drenched in sweat by the time I got to my classroom. I burst through the door just as the final bell rang.

Ms. Foreman stopped me as I started to hurry past her desk. "Good morning, Jordan. How are you?"

"Okay, I guess," I answered. I glanced around the room, looking for Robby.

Ms. Foreman is young, younger than my parents. She's tall and thin and has straight brown hair with streaks of blond in it, bright green eyes, and an awesome smile.

Today she wore a red school T-shirt with EVERGREEN MIDDLE SCHOOL in big blue letters, a denim skirt, and white sneakers. She looks more like a teenager than a teacher, which is probably one reason everyone likes her so much.

"Jordan, I heard you were going to Carnival World," she said. "Did you enjoy it?"

I shrugged. "Not much," I replied.

She made a pouty face with her lips. "Oh, too bad. What went wrong?"

I hesitated. "It's a long story," I said finally.

She smiled. "Oh. Good. You can tell it to everyone this morning."

I blinked. "Excuse me?"

"Did you forget it's oral story day, Jordan? We're telling true stories to the class today. Maybe your story could be about what went wrong at the carnival."

I don't think so, I thought.

"M-maybe," I stammered.

She nodded. "Okay. Go take your seat. I'm going to call on you first."

I opened my mouth to protest. But what was the point?

Tell what happened at the carnival in front of the whole class? I was tense to begin with. But now as I slid into my desk near the back of the room, I felt totally stressed.

Tell what happened? Would anyone believe me? Would everyone just laugh? Would I be teased maybe for the rest of my life?

I dumped my backpack on the floor and kicked

it under my chair. Then I sat there trying to breathe normally, tapping my fingers on the desk. I'm not a fingernail biter. But if I were, I would have chewed them all down to the bone by now.

Ms. Foreman disappeared for a few minutes. Everyone started talking at once. Bernardo stood on his desk and did an insane dance move. He almost fell off the desk twice. Everyone agrees Bernardo is a riot.

He slid back into his seat as Ms. Foreman returned, and the room instantly grew silent. She led a short, brown-haired boy into the room.

His hair fell over his forehead and covered one eye. He had his hands shoved into his jeans pockets. Even from the back of the room, I could see he looked uncomfortable.

"Class, we have a new student," Ms. Foreman announced. She stood behind the kid with her hands on his shoulders. "His name is Liam Nathan."

No, it isn't, I told myself. A stab of fear made my chest ache. I wanted to shout. I wanted to warn Ms. Foreman.

I know who it is. And his name isn't Liam Nathan.

18

I knew I had to say something. Ms. Foreman had just welcomed a *monster* to the classroom. But how could I tell her? If I came right out and said it, she'd never believe me. And the other kids would all be laughing their heads off.

I stared at the boy, studying him. Of course, he looked like a normal kid. Black T-shirt with a red Fender guitar decal on the front, pulled down over faded denim jeans with holes at both knees, low Converse Chuck Taylor sneakers . . .

But he had Robby's hair. And he had Robby's shy smile.

A monster. He's a monster.

I knew the damage he could do. I knew how he could rage out of control. He could hurt people. He was totally dangerous.

How could I warn the teacher?

At the front of the room, Ms. Foreman was still offering the kid her nicest smile. "Welcome to our school, Liam," she said. "I know everyone in our class will give you a very warm welcome."

He nodded and murmured thanks. I could just barely hear him.

"Do you have any questions about our school?" Ms. Foreman asked him.

He pushed the hair off his eyes. "Yes," he said. "When is lunchtime?"

That PROVES it! I thought.

The class burst out laughing, of course. But I didn't laugh. That answer sent a chill down my back. At lunchtime, he would grow into a snarling beast and start hurting people. Maybe wreck the whole school.

I had no choice. I had to warn Ms. Foreman.

I raised my hand high and waved it in the air. "Ms. Foreman? Ms. Foreman?" I shouted.

She turned to me. "No, not yet, Jordan," she said. "We're not telling our true stories yet. I *said* I'd call on you first."

"But—But—" I sputtered.

Then I realized the kid had his eyes locked on me. He trapped me in a cold stare. He saw me for the first time. Robby knew that I was about to tell the teacher the truth about him.

His gaze was like ice. I mean, beyond cruel. I could see he was threatening me, warning me to shut up.

I lowered my hand to the desk. Some kids

were staring at me. Could they see how frightened I was?

"Liam," Ms. Foreman said, pointing at me. "Why don't you take that empty desk next to Jordan?"

Oh noooo.

The kid nodded and came walking down the aisle between the desks. He kept his eyes on me the whole time. He stopped in front of my desk, and I thought he was going to say something.

I thought maybe he was about to warn me to keep my mouth shut. Or threaten to do something terrible if I snitched on him.

But no. He didn't say a word. He gave me one last look with those deep, dark brown eyes. Then edged past me and dropped onto the desk seat beside me.

I turned to the front. I clasped my hands together so he couldn't see they were shaking. I pretended everything was okay. Perfectly normal.

Ms. Foreman sat on the edge of her desk and began talking about the class picnic. We have it on the picnic grounds at Carnival World every year. She said after the picnic, our class could go on some of the rides.

I tried to concentrate on what she was saying. But it was really hard, knowing that a dangerous monster was sitting at the desk next to me and watching my every move.

How could I pretend he wasn't there?

And then when he tapped me on the shoulder, I nearly lost it. I nearly screamed, but somehow I held it in.

He leaned over and whispered in my ear. "Did you bring lunch to school, or do you eat in the cafeteria?"

19

"Uh . . ." I froze. I could still feel the hard tap on my shoulder. His question repeated in my ears.

He was letting me know who he was. And he was warning me that lunch period was going to be a horror show.

"Jordan? Jordan? Earth calling Jordan!"

Ms. Foreman's voice broke through my terrified thoughts. I shook "Liam's" voice from my mind and turned toward her.

"Jordan, didn't you hear me? It's time for our reports. Come up here and tell the class your true story. It's about Carnival World, right?"

"Well . . ." I glanced at "Liam" next to me. What would he do if I told the truth? If I told the story of how we let him escape from the carnival?

Would he attack me?

Probably.

My legs were trembling as I pulled myself to

my feet. My mind was spinning. I started to make my way to the front of the class.

As I turned to face everyone, I decided what to do. I'd tell the true story about the carnival, but I'd make it sound like a joke.

I'd make everyone laugh. That way, Robby would know that I wasn't going to snitch on him.

I shoved my hands into my jeans pockets and rocked back and forth on my shoes. Then I took a couple of deep breaths.

"You'll never guess what happened to me at Carnival World," I started. "I swear this is true." I winked and made a face to make them think I was kidding, that it wasn't true at all.

Then I told them about being trapped in the Tunnel of Fear. I changed this part a little. I made it sound like Karla was totally frightened and I had to be brave to take care of her.

Then I told them how we came out of the tunnel at the back and how the carnival owner gave us candy bars. And then I came to the part where we found the boy sitting in the cage with the sign that said not to feed him.

I grinned and tried to make it seem like I was telling a joke, a made-up story. But my voice was shaky, and kids kept shouting for me to talk louder.

Hey, I was trying to look calm, but I was scared to death. I kept my eyes on "Liam" near the back of the room, and he was watching me with the coldest stare on his face.

Was he warning me not to tell the story? Was he planning to come roaring at me if I told everyone who he was?

It's scary enough to give an oral report in front of the class. But it's a lot scarier to have a dangerous *monster* watching you and listening to your every word.

I hiccupped and everyone laughed.

"Go on, Jordan," Ms. Foreman interrupted. "The story is just getting good."

"I . . . I (*hic*) have the hiccups," I said, faking that last hic. "I'll have to finish (*hic*) tomorrow."

"Sorry. This isn't a miniseries." She handed me a water bottle and watched as I took a long swallow. "Okay. Go on with your story," she said.

"Well . . . Karla and I should have obeyed the sign," I said. "But we felt sorry for the boy, and we gave him a few chunks of candy bar."

"Liam" leaned forward over his desktop. His eyes were wide now. He didn't blink or move. His hands were balled into fists on the desktop.

I knew he wanted me to stop. But I had gone too far. I had told too much of the story.

I forced a laugh. I tried to make it sound like a joke I was making up. I told how the boy started to vomit and how he grew fur and ballooned up till he was enormous.

"He became a roaring monster," I said. "Karla and I should have obeyed the sign. But the candy turned him into a huge, angry creature. And he broke out of the cage and ran through the carnival scaring everyone and—"

Everyone was laughing now. The whole class *did* think it was a joke. Kids were roaring and slapping their desks and hee-hawing and hooting.

Everyone but "Liam." He didn't laugh.

I saw his eyes bulge. His mouth shot open. He let out a cry and jumped to his feet.

Here he comes, I told myself. *I'm dead meat. Here he comes.*

20

I stumbled back against the wall. The laughter stopped as kids saw "Liam" leap to his feet.

His face reddened. His eyes were still bulging.

Ms. Foreman stood up from her desk chair. "Liam?" she called. "What's wrong?"

Everyone turned to look at him. I had my eyes on the door, ready to run out of the room.

"A bee," Liam said. "A bee. It tried to sting me."

He's lying!

Did I say those words or just think them? I was too scared to think straight.

He's lying, Ms. Foreman. He was about to attack me.

"Do you see the bee now?" she asked him.

He shook his head. "I think it flew away."

There was a lot of murmuring and tense mumbling in the room. A lot of kids don't like bees.

Bernardo jumped to his feet, gazing all around. "I'm allergic to bees," he told Ms. Foreman. "My whole body swells up."

"I don't see it," Ms. Foreman said. "Sit down, Bernardo. You too, Liam. It must have flown back out the window."

It took a few minutes to get everyone quiet and settled down. I didn't move. I stood with my back against the wall, my arms crossed, waiting for Ms. Foreman to tell me I could sit down.

Finally, she turned to me. "Jordan, I'm a little confused," she said, squinting at me.

I swallowed. "Confused?"

She nodded. "Yes. That was a very entertaining horror story. I *guess* you'd call it a horror story. A fantasy story, maybe? Very imaginative, very clever."

"Thanks," I said softly.

"But I can't give you a passing grade," she continued. "The assignment was to tell a *true* story—not a made-up story."

I had my eyes on "Liam." He was perched on the edge of his chair, leaning tensely over the desktop. His hands were still clenched into fists.

"But . . . it *was* a true story," I protested.

That made a lot of kids laugh. Ms. Foreman laughed, too.

Then she shook her head. "Nice try. I don't want to give you a failing grade, Jordan. Tell you what. I'll call you up again after everyone else has talked. Then maybe you can tell us a *true* story about the carnival."

"Yeah. Okay," I said. I didn't know what else to say.

I forced a grin onto my face. Like the whole thing was a joke to me. And I kind of strutted back to my seat.

But, believe me, I didn't feel like grinning or strutting. I dropped down beside the monster and kept my eyes on the front of the room. Ms. Foreman called Shonda Fallows to the front. Shonda started to talk about her first horseback riding lesson.

I cradled my head in my hands and pretended to be totally into Shonda's story. But I knew "Liam" had his eye on me.

And sure enough, he tapped me hard on the shoulder again.

I had no choice. I had to turn toward him.

He leaned closer and whispered. "I want to tell you something."

I made a gulping sound. "What?" I whispered.

21

He hesitated. At the front of the class, Shonda was finishing her story. Some kids started to clap.

My skin was tingling again. I tensed my leg muscles, getting ready to run. "What did you want to tell me?"

"I really liked your story," "Liam" said. "I thought it was awesome."

I stared at him. "Thanks," I murmured.

What does he mean by that? What is he trying to tell me?

We both knew his secret. We both knew that I knew who he really was.

He brushed his hair off his eyes. Then he settled back in his seat and turned to the front of the room.

Was he being sarcastic? Was he trying to frighten me?

I didn't know how much longer I could sit there beside the monster without exploding. I *had* to tell Ms. Foreman the truth about him. I had to get over my terror—before he did something horrible.

If people got hurt, it would be my fault.

No. No way. I couldn't let that happen.

I took a deep breath and raised my hand high. I waved it impatiently. "Ms. Foreman? Ms. Foreman?"

My heart was beating so hard in my chest, it made my voice break. I waved my hand high. "Ms. Foreman?"

She didn't hear me. She perched on the edge of her desk again. "I forgot to eat breakfast this morning," she said. "Does anyone have anything in their backpack I could nibble on?"

22

"Huh?" A gasp escaped my throat.

Shonda Fallows began to dig in her backpack. "I think I have something, Ms. Foreman."

No. Wait.

Shonda handed Ms. Foreman a chocolate cupcake.

My breath caught in my throat. I tried to call out a warning, but I was only able to release a squeak.

"Thank you, Shonda. You're a lifesaver," Ms. Foreman said. She carefully peeled the paper off the cupcake. She tossed the paper onto her desk. Then she raised the cupcake in front of her—and jammed the whole thing into her mouth.

She made loud chewing sounds as she mashed the cupcake between her teeth. She began grunting like an animal. Her eyes spun in her head, and she swallowed the mashed-up cupcake with a loud *gulllp*.

"Oh no," I murmured. "Oh no." But I was help-less to do anything, frozen in shock in my chair.

Ms. Foreman leaped to her feet, tossed her head back—and let out a sick, disgusting wet burp. "BLLURRRRRRRRRRPP."

Kids called out, laughed, gasped. Everyone was confused. Who could believe it?

I could.

And, of course, things instantly became more frightening.

The teacher opened her mouth wide, and a thick stream of orange vomit spewed into the air. It splashed over the kids in the front row.

Everyone was screaming now. Shonda raised her backpack over her head, trying to pro-tect herself. But the hot spray of vomit poured over her, soaking the front of her T-shirt and her skirt.

Ms. Foreman stretched her arms out wide as the fur began to sprout. In seconds, her face dis-appeared behind the thick covering of green, prickly fur. Her arms became furry gorilla arms. Green fur poked out from her clothes.

Her body stretched up toward the ceiling. She twisted her head and roared as she grew. In sec-onds, she was an ugly, furious monster. A monster I knew well.

Without realizing it, I was out of my seat. "Stop!" I cried. "Robby—stop right now!"

In a fever of fright, I hurtled toward the creature. I leaped off the floor and wrapped my hands around his waist, trying to tackle him, desperate to bring him down.

"Ohhh!" I cried out when he didn't budge. It was like trying to tackle a mountain.

Stunned, I shut my eyes. My hands slid off him and I hit the floor hard. Bounced once. Struggled to get back on my feet.

With a roar, the monster slapped both paws against my chest. Pain shot down my whole body. I started to slump back to the floor.

But he grabbed me by the front of my T-shirt. Held me up with both paws—and *ripped* my shirt in two.

"NOOOO!" I screamed, twisting and squirming, frantic to get away.

Why had I attacked the creature? What was I *thinking*?

I spun free—but for only a second. I felt the steel-hard fingers wrap around my waist. And with a hard tug, the monster tore my jeans away.

I staggered back. In my underpants. I stumbled, shaking my head, dazed.

The room echoed with terrified screams.

The monster tilted back his head in a hoarse animal roar. He swept his hand over the desk, sending everything smashing, clattering to the floor. He lifted a tall bookshelf off the wall and heaved it across the room. Kids screamed and ducked away as it crashed over desks, spilling books everywhere.

With another roar, he overturned the aquarium, sending a lake of water over the floor, yellow and red fish flapping helplessly at my feet.

"Stop it, Robby!" I screamed, finding my voice again. "Stop it!"

He heaved the aquarium against the wall. It shattered, and shards of glass flew into the air, sending kids ducking and diving for cover.

I spun away, trying to avoid the flying glass. When I turned back, the monster had raided someone's backpack. He held a sandwich in a sandwich bag and stuffed the whole thing into his mouth. The plastic bag poked from his mouth as he chewed. He swallowed the sandwich and the bag.

Then, ignoring the screams and cries that filled the room, he let out another long, wet burp. Swung around. Shoved me out of the way. And took a running dive out the open window.

I tried to force my heartbeats to slow. I was gasping for air. I saw Liam at the back of the room. He was standing beside his desk, hugging himself, trembling.

I had been so wrong about him. But I didn't have time to think about it.

I turned when I heard a voice at the classroom door. Ms. Foreman stood there in her jacket, her briefcase in hand. The *real* Ms. Foreman.

"Sorry I'm late, everyone," she said. "Car trouble."

She squinted at me. Her mouth dropped open when she saw that I was standing there in my underpants.

And then her eyes nearly flew out of her head. "Oh, good heavens! What *happened* here?"

23

A few minutes later, I was on the phone. "Mom, please hurry. Bring me jeans and a T-shirt. Can you get here fast?"

"Jordan, what happened to your clothes?"

"It's a long story. I promise I'll tell you every-thing when you get here."

"But what are you wearing now?"

"Nothing! I mean, just my underpants. Mom—please—can I explain later? Ms. Foreman gave me her jacket to cover me up. But things are a little . . . weird."

Yes. Things were weird at my school. For one thing, there were blue-uniformed cops every-where you looked. And a line of kids outside Miss Lyons's office. She's the principal, and she wanted to talk to every kid in our class before we were allowed to go home. And every parent.

The parents waited outside Miss Lyons's office, too. They were all shaking their heads in disbelief when they found out what had happened.

A monster at Evergreen Middle School? Impossible!

A monster who made himself look like Ms. Foreman and then spewed hot vomit all over kids, trashed the classroom, and escaped out the window?

Just how impossible *is* that?

I saw cops scratching their heads. And I heard the murmured protests and cries of horror from the worried parents. Maybe some of them didn't believe it. But everyone in my class saw it happen.

The story of the escaped monster was out. Of course, there was one piece of it I didn't tell. One part I didn't want anyone to know.

And that was the part where *I* was the one who let Robby out. I was the one who let him escape. It was all my fault.

And while we all know I'm not the bravest person on the planet, I felt like I should be the one to do something to help capture him.

But what could I do?

I changed into the clothes Mom brought me in the boys' room. Then Miss Lyons ushered us into her office. "Sorry you had to come rushing to school," she told Mom. "It's been quite a day."

"No problem," Mom answered, taking a seat at

the table in Miss Lyons's back office. "I had to make sure Jordan and Karla were okay."

"Everyone is okay," the principal said. She sighed. "But just barely."

Lyons is the perfect name for her. She has a pile of orange-brown hair that looks a lot like a lion's mane. She's big and she moves very fast, taking long lion strides. And her dark eyes are wide and round. She looks as if she's always studying you, looking for prey.

"This is Officer Hayes," she said, pointing to a young cop who sat with his back to the window. He nodded in greeting. He had very short blond hair, bright blue eyes the size of marbles in his narrow, pale face, and a thin-lipped, serious expression that seemed to be frozen on his face.

I glanced out the window behind Officer Hayes. I could see more parents arriving at the parking lot, hurrying from their cars, tense expressions on their faces.

Mom clasped her hands tightly together on the tabletop. She was biting her lips. She always does that when she's really stressed.

She didn't let Miss Lyons ask a question. She began the conversation. "The monster was in our house," she said. "He wrecked our entire kitchen."

Miss Lyons blinked. "Then you saw him, too?"

"No," Mom replied. "He ran off just before my

93

husband and I returned home. Jordan was the only one at home."

"Can *you* describe him, Jordan?" Hayes chimed in. He had an iPad in front of him on the table. He used two fingers to type on it. "It's a shame no one snapped a photo of him. So I'm asking everyone in your class to describe him."

"Well . . ." I started. "When he's a monster, he looks kind of like a giant bear. He gets covered in green fur, and he grows big bear paws and a bear snout."

Hayes typed on the iPad keyboard.

"But he usually doesn't look like a monster," I explained. "When we saw him at Carnival World, he looked like a boy. About my age. He said his name was Robby."

Miss Lyons gasped. Officer Hayes stopped typing and raised his blue eyes at me. "You saw him at Carnival World?"

I nodded. "He escaped from there. He got out of his cage and ran away. He . . . he followed us home."

"He looked like a boy when he came to your house?" Miss Lyons asked.

I nodded. "Then when I fed him, he turned into a monster."

Hayes jumped to his feet. He grabbed his iPad from the table. "Got to get to Carnival World right away," he said. "I've run into the owner before. His name is Ferber. Maybe Ferber can help us round up this boy or monster or whatever he is."

He hurried from the office. Miss Lyons leaned over the tabletop and tapped her fingers on the polished wood. "I have a few more questions," she said.

I didn't hear what she said next. Something outside her office window caught my eye. A blur of movement. The sun was in my eyes and I squinted hard, trying to focus.

And I screamed when I saw the huge, green-furred monster in the parking lot. "Noooo! Look! Look!" I cried, pointing frantically.

Miss Lyons twisted in her chair to see where I was pointing. And the three of us stared out the window, mouths open, as the monster went berserk.

The squeal of metal against metal was deafening as he ripped the driver's door off a police patrol car. Roaring at the sky, he heaved the door across the parking lot. It crashed against a fence.

Then the huge creature leaned into the car and, grunting loudly, pulling and twisting, his big fur-covered shoulders rippling, he jerked the front seat out. Pulled it out in both paws and sent it flying over a row of cars.

"Oh, wow," I murmured. "It . . . It's like a horror movie."

Mom and Miss Lyons were on their feet. "The

police are searching the back of the building," Miss Lyons said. "They must not hear what's going on."

And then the monster turned. He narrowed his eyes and peered into the principal's office window. He stood perfectly still for a long moment, staring at us. Staring. Watching us watching him.

Then he uttered an animal roar and came striding toward the school building.

"He—he's coming for us!" I stammered.

24

Her eyes wide with fright, Mom swung away from the table and lurched toward the office door. But her foot caught a chair leg, and she fell to her knees on the carpet.

Miss Lyons and I froze in place as the creature loomed bigger and bigger in the window. And then it seemed as if the sun had gone out. The room turned black as he blocked all the light.

I gasped. Was he going to leap into the room? Was he about to attack us?

No. A huge fist shot into the room, shattering the window with a deafening crash. I ducked. Too late. A blast of glass shards sent me staggering back against the wall.

Then the sunlight came pouring back through the window as the monster moved on. I could hear his thunderous footsteps from somewhere outside, but I couldn't see him. I shook my head, sending pieces of glass falling to the floor. I brushed glass off the front of my shirt.

Mom groaned. "I think I twisted my ankle." Miss Lyons and I hurried to help her up.

Outside, we heard the shouts of police officers. Finally! I saw two officers running toward the ripped-apart patrol car.

One cop right outside our smashed window had a phone pressed to his mouth. "We need backup here!" he cried. "The monster is real—and it's big and angry."

A brief pause. Then he screamed into the phone: "You *heard* me. A monster is going berserk here. No. I don't know the code number for that. Do *you*?"

Cops were running around all over the parking lot. One of them had the patrol car door in his hands. He was shaking his head in disbelief.

"I'm going to have to keep the kids in school till we get an all-clear from the police," Miss Lyons said. "Parents don't have to stay. Unless you want to."

She started toward the door. "Are you okay, Mrs. Keppler? I have to talk to the other parents."

Leaning on a chair, Mom tested her ankle. "I'm okay," she said. She and I followed Miss Lyons out into the hall.

Liam and his mother were next in line. We nodded to each other in greeting. "Hey, Jordan, how's it going?" he asked.

I shrugged in reply.

"It's Liam's first day of school," his mother told Miss Lyons. "How could this happen on his very first day?"

I didn't hear the answer. Mom and I walked through the crowd to my classroom. I thought about Liam. I felt bad that I'd suspected him of being the monster. He seemed like a nice kid now.

He probably felt totally awkward being in a new school for the first time. And there I was, raising my hand, planning to tell Ms. Foreman that he was a monster.

That would have been seriously embarrassing. Especially since SHE was the monster.

"Listen, Jordan," Mom said, taking my arm. "I took the morning off, but I have to get to work now. I want you to call me as soon as they say it's safe for you to leave the school."

"No problem," I said.

"I'll come pick you up—"

"If they say the monster has left, Karla and I can walk home," I said. "It's only four blocks. We'll be okay."

"Call me when you leave school, and call me when you get home," Mom said. "Don't forget."

"No worries."

She kissed my cheek. "Love you." Then she turned and hobbled out the front door.

The police were still in our classroom. So, one by one, kids in Ms. Foreman's class were

99

gathering in the library after their meetings with Miss Lyons. Ms. Foreman tried to lead a discussion about being afraid and how to get over it.

But no one was in the mood to talk. I think we were all listening for the monster to return.

So Ms. Foreman said it was quiet reading time. And we all found library books and read silently—until a little after four o'clock. That's when the police gave the all-clear. They couldn't find the monster anywhere.

"Be very careful, everyone," Ms. Foreman said. She stood at the door as we filed out and said nice things to each of us. She was trying to be brave and act normal. But I saw her hands trembling, and her face was totally pale.

I met up with Karla in our usual place in the playground, and we crossed the street, heading home. Billowing gray clouds covered the sun, and the air began to grow cold. It felt like rain was coming.

"Do you think Robby is still hanging around?" Karla asked. "Is he going to be waiting in our kitchen, hoping for an after-school snack?"

I shrugged. "Beats me." I kept darting my eyes all around. "He's totally tricky. He fooled everyone, Karla. Everyone thought he was Ms. Foreman."

Karla shivered. "And he trashed the room?"

I nodded. "I think he's getting more and more

violent. He smashed his fist through Miss Lyons's office window."

"Maybe if he knows the police are after him, he'll go to another town," she said.

"Maybe," I murmured. But I didn't really believe it.

We stopped at the corner to let an SUV filled with kids roll by. I felt a cold drop of rain on my forehead. "We're going to get drenched," I said.

Karla shifted her backpack on her shoulders. "Did you remember to call Mom?"

"Oh. No. I forgot." I started to reach for my phone when I felt a tap on my shoulder. "Hey!" I cried out in surprise. Normally, I wouldn't have reacted like that but, things were tense.

I turned and stared at Liam. He had a gray hoodie pulled up over his head. His hair fell over one eye. He looked very pale in the gray light.

"Hi," he said. "Can I . . . can I walk with you? I don't really know the streets that well."

"No problem," I replied. Liam didn't want to say it, but I could see he was frightened. I introduced him to Karla. "Liam just started school here today."

Karla grinned. "You had an *awesome* first day!"

All three of us laughed, but it was a grim kind of laughter.

The wind swept Liam's hood back. His hair flew off his face. I could see the fear in his eyes.

"Where do you live?" Karla asked him.

He pointed down the street. "On Blackwood. I think it's a block or two from here."

"We'll show you," I said. We started to walk.

"I've never been so scared just walking home," Karla confessed. "But . . . maybe the police captured him. Maybe we're all safe now."

Two older kids from the high school came roaring up on bikes and brushed past us, nearly knocking the three of us off the sidewalk. They laughed as we screamed in surprise.

"Very funny, guys," Karla muttered.

Liam shook his head. "It's too dangerous here," he said.

We walked another half block. I was debating whether or not to tell him what I thought when I'd first seen him this morning. Finally, I decided to go ahead and say it.

"Can I tell you something funny?" I started. "You won't believe this, Liam. But when you came into our class this morning and Ms. Foreman introduced you, I thought *you* were the monster."

Liam laughed. His eyes flashed. "I *am* the monster!" he said.

25

I laughed. I thought he was joking.

But then he grabbed Karla and me by the backs of our necks and shoved us off the sidewalk—and I knew it wasn't a joke.

His strength still surprised me. With his left hand wrapped around Karla's neck, he lifted her off the ground.

We both kicked and twisted and thrashed and screamed. But the monster held his grasp. He pushed us up someone's front lawn. And as the rain started to come down hard, he forced us through their open garage door and into a small, cluttered garage.

"Let us go! What are you going to do to us?" Karla screamed.

He forced us to the back wall and then loosened his grasp. My neck ached and throbbed from his tight hold on it. My legs suddenly felt weak as I stared at him, unable to force back my fright.

"Where's the *real* Liam?" I cried.

He brushed the hair off his eyes. "How should I know? He probably went home after school. I'm sure he's safe at home with his mommy."

"But—you look and sound just like him," I said. "How do you do that?"

A sneer spread over his lips. "I don't know. It's just what I can do. We all have our talents— right?"

"Let us go!" Karla cried. She seemed more angry than frightened. Karla grabbed a lawn hoe off the garage floor. She gripped the handle and started to swing it in front of Liam. "Back off!" she cried. "I mean it. Go away!"

He laughed. "You're kidding, right? Put that down, Karla. Did you forget I'm a monster? I can *hurt* you!"

She gave it one more swing. Then she heaved it against the garage wall. "Why don't you go away, Robby?" she shouted. "Why are you always picking on *us*?"

Robby's smile faded. "You let me out," he said, lowering his voice. "You are responsible for me."

"No!" I cried. "We can't be. We can't—"

"You have to start taking better care of me," he said. "I need more attention from you. I need more. Do you understand?"

"No. I don't understand," I said. "We didn't mean to let you out. We didn't know you were a monster."

"What do you want us to do?" Karla demanded. "What are you talking about? What do you need from us?"

"Food," he answered. "I need food."

"We can't keep giving you food," I said. "Every time we give you food, you go berserk and—"

"I'm just like you. I need food to stay alive," he said, locking his stare on me. "Don't you understand? I need a lot of food. I get very hungry. I can't help it. I'm a nice guy, but I have some issues I have to deal with. In the meantime, I need you to feed me—a lot."

"Giving you food is too dangerous," I said.

He pushed me against the garage wall. "You don't have a choice, Jordan," he growled. "You're going to feed me every night. Every night, you're going to bring me a big, heaping plate of food."

"N-no, I can't," I stammered. "No way. I—"

He brought his face up close to mine. He still looked like Liam. But his eyes turned fiery red, like an enraged animal.

"Did you forget that I'm a *monster*?" he snarled. "I can do *terrible things* to you both."

"You have to listen to reason," Karla chimed in. "We can't bring you big plates of food every night. Our parents will never allow it."

"Why should I care about your parents?" he snapped. "That's *your* problem."

"But they'll catch us. They'll stop us," I said.

He stood there breathing hard, pressing me against the wall. "Okay," he said finally. "Okay, I have a better idea. Let's go."

"Huh? Go *where*?" I said.

"To your house. You're inviting me to dinner."

26

Karla and I followed him out of the garage. The rain had turned to a light drizzle. The afternoon sun was trying to poke through the clouds.

"We can't do this," Karla whispered. "We can't do this to Mom and Dad."

"What choice do we have?" I whispered back.

Robby spun around. "Did I forget to mention that I have superhearing? I can hear every word you whisper."

I nodded. I didn't know what to say.

"Don't worry about your parents," he said. "Just get me fed."

"You trashed our kitchen," I started. "You—"

He narrowed his eyes at me. "I'll be on my best behavior. I promise. There won't be any trouble."

"You said that before," I told him. "And then—"

He raised his right hand. "I swear. My best behavior." He motioned for us to keep walking.

"Tell your parents I'm Liam Nathan. I'm the new kid in school, and that's why you invited me for dinner."

"But, Robby—"

"They'll be proud of you for wanting to welcome a new kid. You'll see."

Karla and I exchanged worried glances. There was no way we could get out of doing this. We were trapped. We just had to believe Robby when he swore he'd be on his best behavior.

He thinks we're responsible for him now. Does this mean he'll NEVER go away?

That was my frightening thought as we walked home. I didn't dare say it to Karla—since Robby could hear every whisper.

If only I could take out my phone and dial 911. I could get the police to come arrest him.

But why would they? He looked just like Liam. The cops would never believe he was the monster.

Maybe he'll keep his word. Maybe tonight won't be a disaster . . .

A few minutes later, I was in our living room, introducing him to Mom and Dad. "Mom, you already met Liam in school today. Remember? Today was his first day?"

Mom clapped her hands to her cheeks. "Oh, what a terrible day to start. You must have been so frightened, Liam."

He nodded. "It was very scary. I—I couldn't breathe for a moment when Ms. Foreman started to change into a monster."

"Unbelievable," Dad murmured. "Just unbelievable."

"My mom hurried to school," he continued. "You met her, Mrs. Keppler. She said she was sorry we moved here."

He's a seriously good liar, I thought. *My parents totally believe him.*

"Where is your house?" Dad asked Liam.

"On Blackwood," he answered. "But we're just renting. My dad is trying to get a new job."

"What does he do?" Dad asked.

Robby shrugged. "He's some kind of engineer."

Major lying.

"Well, welcome to our house, Liam," Mom said. "I know you've had a tough day, as we all have. So it's nice to have you here."

His eyes opened wide. "When do we eat?" he demanded.

SLAPPY HERE, EVERYONE . . .

Haha. Robby is a great dinner guest. He'll eat everything they put in front of him—including the family dog!

He's so hungry, he'll eat everything on his plate—and yours. When he leaves, you won't have to clean up—because he'll eat the dishes, too! Hahaha.

Sure, he has a little "vomit-on-everyone" problem. But no one is perfect, right?

I had a beautiful dinner party last week. The guest of honor was ME, of course. Know why the dinner conversation was so brilliant? Because I was talking to MYSELF! Hahaha.

Okay. Let's get back to Jordan and Karla's house and see if dinner is a big hit. Or, should I say a SMASH? Hahaha.

27

The rain clouds had floated away, and the evening sky was clear. A warm breeze blew through our backyard. Dad decided we'd have a barbecue.

He piled hamburgers and hot dogs on the grill. Mom, Karla, and I sat on wicker chairs on the patio and watched him move the food around over the charcoal.

Karla and I love barbecues. The aroma of meat and the crackling of food on the grill is my favorite. But we couldn't enjoy the dinner tonight, and we sure couldn't relax.

The fake Liam sat across from Mom and kept telling her lies about his old school and his old hometown. And all the while, he had his eyes on the grill. And he couldn't hide his hungry expression as the meat sizzled and browned.

Karla and I knew he was a monster. And we knew what happened to him when he ate. We both had our fingers crossed. Were we in terrible danger? What would he do if he *didn't* get fed? And if he *did* eat . . . Whoa!

He seemed to be getting more and more violent. Would he hurt us? Would he hurt our whole family?

We were both so tense, we could barely speak. We just sat there watching that hungry look in his eyes and listening to his made-up stories.

"Almost ready," Dad announced. "How do you like your hamburgers, Liam? I like mine burnt black. How about you?"

Liam grinned. "I like them *every* way," he said.

Dad chuckled. But the answer sent chills down my back.

While Dad worked his spatula magic, the three of us kids helped Mom set the picnic table. Our patio stretches along the back of our house. So we have room for a picnic table, a barbecue grill, and even a nice big hammock.

When Mom went into the house to get napkins, Karla and I pulled Liam to the side of the garage. He twisted himself free from us. "What's your problem?" he snapped.

"You *know* our problem," I said. "It's you."

"Are you going to keep your promise?" Karla demanded.

He squinted at her. "Promise?"

"You *know* what we're talking about," I said

112

angrily. "You promised if we brought you home to dinner, you'd be on your best behavior."

He tilted his head to one side. "I *did*?"

"Stop playing games," I snapped. "What's going to happen when we sit down to eat? Are you going to behave?"

He sneered at me. "Don't worry about it, Jordan," he replied. "No worries. Really."

He saw Dad watching us. In a loud voice, Liam said, "That was so nice of you both to invite me. We all had a tense day. It was terrible. Now I'm so happy to be here."

What a fake.

Liam turned away from us and went walking toward the grill. "Can I help you, Mr. Keppler?" he asked.

He didn't wait for my Dad to answer. He grabbed a sizzling hot hamburger off the grill— in his bare hands! And he shoved the whole thing into his mouth.

Mom and Dad both cried out in shock.

Karla and I froze in horror. Liam's words rang in my ears: *I'll be on my best behavior.*

Yikes.

Dad jerked the spatula high as Liam grabbed a couple of burning hot dogs off the grill and stuffed them into his mouth, chewing frantically.

"Liam—what are you *doing*?" Mom screamed.

Dad stumbled back and the spatula flew from his hands. "Stop! This is *crazy*! You'll burn yourself!"

Liam lowered his face to the grill and gobbled up a hamburger with his teeth—like a dog!

The smoke curled around his face. And when he lifted his head, his cheeks were fiery red. And he opened his mouth wide and began to shoot orange vomit over the grill.

"NOOOOOOO!"

"HELLLLLP!"

Mom and Dad were shrieking in horror. Karla and I knew what was coming. And we knew we were helpless to stop it.

The monster spewed thick orange vomit over the picnic table. Then he turned his head and splashed the disgusting orange liquid over my mom.

She screamed and covered her head with both hands. Too late.

I watched Liam begin to change. Saw the ugly green fur poke out of his skin. Saw his face become a snarling creature face as he grew taller ... taller. He rose up over us, snarling, grunting, vomit dribbling down the front of his green fur.

"It—it's the MONSTER!" Dad shouted, his eyes wide with horror. "You two brought home the monster!"

Robby slid another hamburger off the grill and shoved it into his mouth. Chewing noisily, he grabbed the side of the barbecue grill—and heaved it over.

The grill clattered onto its side. Hamburgers and hot dogs toppled off, and the grill tray clanged to the stone patio. Red-hot charcoal tumbled over Dad's shoes. He uttered a cry and stumbled back.

The charcoal spread over the patio. "Get the fire extinguisher!" Mom screamed.

But Karla and I were watching Robby as he took off, running toward the neighbors' yard, monster head tilted back, roaring at the sky.

"Don't let him get away!" Dad screamed.

Dad took off, lowering his shoulder like a football tackle and running hard. "Stop!" he screamed. "Stop right there!"

The monster turned and snarled at him, raking his big claws angrily in the air. But Dad kept running.

Karla and I chased after him.

"No!" I screamed. "Dad—don't! Dad—stop! Nooooo. Stop!"

28

Dad ran up behind the galloping monster and took a running leap. Dad's feet left the ground and he spread his arms to bring the creature down in a flying tackle.

"Oh noooo." A cry escaped my lips as I watched Dad miss. The monster darted ahead, and Dad smashed facedown into the grass.

He hit hard. He made an "Oooof" sound. The impact must have knocked his breath out. He didn't move.

Mom was using the fire extinguisher on the burning coals. Karla and I went running toward Dad. But we stopped when we saw the monster spin around.

He froze, his furry arms raised high. He stared at us.

Dad groaned, still flat on his stomach on the grass.

The big creature stepped over him, then began

to trot, snapping his jaw, making ugly grunting sounds.

"Look out!" I screamed. "He's coming *back*!"

His paws thundered loudly over our lawn as he roared back. He lowered his head menacingly and made a bleating sound like an angry goat.

"Don't hurt us!" Karla screamed, covering her face with her hands.

"Stop! Go away! Go away!" I cried.

Wheezing loudly, he burst onto the patio. I gave Karla a shove to the side. Then I scrambled out of his way. But he wasn't interested in us.

He made a dive for the picnic table. Then he swept his paw around the plate of hamburger buns. He tilted the plate to his open mouth—and swallowed the buns with a loud *gullllp*.

He grabbed the bag of hot dog buns and shoved it into his mouth without opening it. Then he raised his head and opened his mouth in a throaty, gross "Urrrrrrrp."

He glanced at Karla, then at me, making whispered grunts. Maybe he was thanking us for dinner. I don't know. I just wanted him to leave.

He turned and trotted over the charcoal scattered on the patio, crunching it under his paws. We watched him until he disappeared around the side of the house. Then the three of us hurried to help Dad.

He was just climbing to his feet, taking deep

breaths and working his arms back and forth, testing them.

"Are you okay?" Mom wrapped her arms around his waist.

He blinked several times, dazed. "I . . . I guess." Then he squinted across the backyard. "Where did he go? Did the monster leave?"

I nodded. "For now."

Dad turned to me. "What do you mean? You think he'll come back?"

"He might," Karla said.

"He said we're responsible for him," I told Dad. "Because we let him out of the carnival."

Dad narrowed his eyes, thinking hard. "The carnival . . ." he murmured.

"The carnival owner," Mom said. "He'll know how to capture him. We have to go back there—right now. The monster is that man's property, right? So he'll have to know what has to be done to capture him and bring him back to the carnival."

And suddenly, I had a flash. Suddenly, I knew just what to do.

"I have a plan," I said. "I have a plan that will definitely work."

29

Manny Ferber greeted us at the front gate to Carnival World. He was dressed again in denim overalls and a plaid lumberjack shirt. His shirt was stained and one sleeve was torn.

His eyes were bloodshot, and his long hair looked greasy and fell in tangles over his face. Patches of beard clung to his cheeks.

"Have you seen him?" he demanded. "Have you? I haven't been able to sleep. Look at me. I'm a total wreck. I saw what he did at your school. I'm so frightened of the damage he could cause."

"We saw him again," I said.

Ferber pulled the gate open. "Come in. Come in. The park is empty. We don't open for another hour. We have some time to talk. Can you tell me—?"

"Let's get serious," my dad interrupted. "Do you know how to capture him or not?"

Ferber shrugged. "Not really. I—"

"He nearly set my backyard on fire," Dad said. "He could destroy our entire neighborhood."

Ferber shook his head sadly. "I never should have brought him here. I . . . I thought I could control him. But . . ."

I glanced past him to the carnival grounds. People were setting up their food booths. Loud piano music floated out of a large tent. A man in a clown costume was wobbly, practicing walking on tall stilts.

Happy people. They weren't worried about a dangerous monster.

A monster I let out. A monster I was responsible for.

I turned back to Ferber. "I have a plan," I said. "I think it might work."

Everyone stared at me.

"I'll try anything," Ferber said. "I'm completely desperate."

I pointed to the picnic grounds at the side of the entrance building. "Can we take a look over there?"

Ferber nodded. He started to lead the way. It was a wide, grassy area with three long rows of wooden picnic tables. Behind the tables stood an enormous charcoal grill the size of a furnace.

Tall evergreen trees formed a wall between the picnic section and the carnival grounds. And several of them dotted the area around the wooden picnic tables.

"My class picnic is going to be here," I said. "If we can get Robby to come here, you can capture him and put him back in his cage."

Ferber brushed a strand of hair from his eyes. "Get him to come here? How?"

I didn't answer. I was studying the picnic tables. I found what I was looking for and led everyone down the row of tables. I stopped at a table in front of a wide evergreen tree.

"I'll eat my picnic lunch here at this table," I said. "Robby will show up. He'll come because he thinks it's my job to feed him."

They all stared at me. They didn't understand what I had in mind.

"So you'll feed him at your class picnic and turn him into a monster?" Karla asked, puzzled.

I shook my head. "No. Let me finish. Mr. Ferber, you can hide behind this big evergreen tree. You can probably hide a couple of workers back there with you."

He turned and stepped behind the wide tree. "Yes. Plenty of room."

"And do you have a big net?" I asked. "I'll get Robby here. He'll be drooling over the food I'm going to spread all over the table. Before he can eat any of it, you jump out, throw the net over him, and you've got him."

Ferber's eyes flashed. "I like it. It might work, Jordan. And you know what? I could hide the cage behind that tree." He pointed to another tree nearby. "That way, my workers and I wouldn't have to drag him very far."

Karla looked from the picnic table to the tree. "Do you really think it will work?"

I grinned. "Will Robby be able to resist a big picnic lunch? I don't think so."

Dad patted me on the shoulder. "Jordan, you just may be a genius."

But that night I lay wide awake in my bed thinking of all the things that could go wrong.

What if Robby grabbed some food and ate it before Ferber could throw the net over him? Would a net hold a roaring monster?

What if Robby disguised himself as one of my friends and ate some of the food before I realized it was him?

What if he escaped from the net before they could drag him to the cage?

What if it rained and the class picnic was called off?

There were so many things that could go wrong. As I tossed and turned and stared at the shifting shadows on my bedroom ceiling, I didn't feel like a genius.

I felt like someone who could be in terrible danger.

But . . . there was one thing I *wasn't* worried about. I knew Robby would be back.

And sure enough, just as I began to fade into

sleep, a loud *tap* on my bedroom window made me sit up, wide awake.

Another *tap*.

I pushed the covers down and lowered my feet to the floor. Moonlight filled my bedroom window, making it glow like silver.

I crossed the room to the window and pushed it open.

"Hi, Robby," I said.

30

He looked pale under the moonlight. His light brown hair fell over one eye. The yellow light made the freckles on his cheeks appear green.

"I just came to apologize," he said softly. He stared in at me, his expression sad, almost shy.

I didn't say anything. I just gazed out at him.

"I'm sorry things got out of control," he said.

"Out of control?" I replied. "You knocked over the barbecue. You could have burned down my house."

"I feel really bad about that," he said, lowering his eyes. "Seriously. Your parents were so nice to me, and I . . . I went and ruined the whole barbecue."

"Please go away," I said. "I have to get some sleep."

"I just came to apologize," he said. "It won't happen again. I promise."

"You don't keep your promises," I replied.

He shook his head. "No. This time I mean it. I promise it won't happen again."

"Please," I said. "I have to get some sleep. Tomorrow is our big class picnic."

His eyes flashed. He suddenly appeared alert. "Picnic? Really? Where?"

"It's at Carnival World," I told him. "There's going to be hot dogs and pizza and all kinds of sandwiches and then cookies and cupcakes."

I knew his mouth was watering. His eyes were wide with excitement.

"You'd better stay away, Robby," I said. "Don't ruin it for everybody."

I could see him thinking hard about it. My plan had started to work. Now he knew about the picnic. And I knew there was *no way* he would miss it.

"Do you have any food?" he asked in a tiny, pleading voice. "I'm really hungry."

"No," I said. "No food. Been there, done that."

"Just a little snack?" he asked. "Something to chew on till breakfast?"

"Good night," I said, and I shoved the window shut.

I was halfway back to bed when I heard a *tap*

on the window behind me. I stopped and listened. Another *tap*.

I walked back to the window and pulled it open.

"Good night," Robby said. "Just wanted to say good night. And don't worry, Jordan. I'll stay away from your picnic tomorrow."

31

"You look terrible," Karla said. "Didn't you get any sleep?"

"How could I sleep?" I said. "I'm totally stressed out of my mind, and I'm going to be a wreck until Robby is captured."

"Your plan is genius," she said. "It's going to work. I know it is."

I stared at her. "You're lying—aren't you?"

She shrugged. "Maybe. Trying to be positive, you know?"

We were walking to school on a warm, sunny morning. The air smelled sweet. Birds tweeted in the trees. Nearly summer, but how could I enjoy any of it?

"If Robby shows up and grabs some food and turns into a monster, people could get hurt," I said. I held her back as a yellow school bus rumbled past. "Why don't you ever watch for traffic before you cross?" I scolded.

She grinned. "I like to live dangerously. Like you."

I forced a smile. I didn't feel like talking at all.

By the time my class climbed off the school bus at Carnival World for our picnic, I was a trembling, shuddering wreck. Every loud voice made me jump. Every time someone moved toward me quickly, I wanted to scream. Every shadow on the grass made my heart skip a beat.

I kept telling myself to chill out. *Robby will be caught. Your plan is a good one. It's going to work. You're going to be okay.*

Before I got into the long line at the food table, I checked the evergreen tree behind the picnic table. *Yes!* Ferber was in place, huddled behind the tree with two of his workers. I saw a big rope net piled on the grass beside them.

They were ready. I flashed Ferber a thumbs-up, then hurried to get in line. I piled two hot dogs on my plate and big mounds of macaroni and coleslaw. I wanted the plate to look really tempting to Robby when he showed up.

"Wow, Jordan, you must be hungry today!" Ms. Foreman said, handing me a bottle of juice.

"Yeah. I'm having a growth spurt," I said. Awkward. But I didn't know what else to say.

I turned to carry my plate to the table near the evergreen tree. The tables were already filled with kids eating, talking, and laughing. At one table, kids were squirting each other with the ketchup and mustard dispensers. I saw Ms. Foreman trotting over to stop them.

I was nearly to my table when someone bumped me hard from behind. I stumbled forward and my food plate went flying from my hands.

"Whoa!" Somehow, I managed to catch it in midair—without spilling anything.

I spun around and stared at my friend Bernardo. He had a grin on his face. "Sorry, Jordan. Guess I don't know my own strength." His plate was piled even higher than mine.

"Where you sitting?" Bernardo asked. "I'll sit with you."

I stared hard at him. Was it really Bernardo? Or was it Robby?

No way to tell.

He followed me to the table in front of the evergreen tree. I set my plate down and squeezed onto the wooden bench. Bernardo—if it *was* Bernardo—dropped down across from me.

I could hear Ferber stirring behind the tree. Was he raising the net?

Wait, I thought. *Don't bring the net out yet. This may really be Bernardo.*

"This is awesome," Bernardo said. "We should do this every week. Right?"

"Uh . . . right," I answered.

"Hurry up and eat," he said. "When we're finished we can go on the rides. Want to go into the Tunnel of Fear?"

"I don't *think* so," I said. My eyes were on his food plate.

Should I give the signal—wave my arm—so Ferber and his guys could run out with the net raised? If it was Robby sitting across from me, and he ate some of the food, it would be too late.

Bernardo raised a hot dog off his plate. "Hey, Jordan—how come you're not eating?"

I couldn't tell him my stomach was tied in a dozen knots. *No way* I could eat even a bread crumb!

What should I do? What should I do?

Bernardo answered the question for me. He jammed the hot dog into his mouth and began to chew up big bites. Then he swallowed a chunk of macaroni and washed it down with a long slug of apple juice.

I gritted my teeth. Gripped the bench with both hands. And waited for him to explode in a gusher of orange vomit.

32

But Bernardo didn't vomit and grow green fur and turn into a roaring monster. All he did was gobble the rest of the food on his plate and go back for a second helping.

Bernardo was definitely Bernardo.

Okay. But could I relax now? Of course not. I tried to nibble at a hot dog, but my mouth was so dry I couldn't swallow.

Bernardo finished his second helping and ran off to join the kickball game some kids had started in the playground next to the picnic area.

I sat on the bench, pretending to eat so no one would get suspicious. And I waited for Robby to show up.

I knew he would. I'd told him all about the picnic last night. How could he resist?

So I waited there. The sun was in my eyes. I began to sweat.

But I waited . . . and waited.

And waited.

The picnic tables were nearly empty now. The other kids in my class had finished their lunch. They were playing kickball or just hanging out in the playground area. Ms. Foreman was helping the carnival staff clean up.

"Hey, Jordan—what's up?" Mr. Ferber called in a loud whisper from behind the tree. "Where is he?"

I shrugged. "Beats me," I said. "He's coming. I know he's coming."

I waited some more. And then some more.

I shut my eyes against the bright sunlight. And waited some more.

A hand tapped my shoulder.

I jumped. "Hey—!"

Ms. Foreman gazed down at me. "Jordan? Aren't you feeling well?"

"Uh . . . I'm fine," I said.

She picked up my plate. "You hardly ate. Well, go join the others. We're going to go on some of the rides."

I watched her carry my food plate to the trash can. Then I climbed slowly to my feet. "Sorry," I murmured to Ferber behind the tree. "I really thought he would come."

"This is a big disappointment," he replied.

Maybe Robby knew it was a trap, I suddenly thought.

But how could he? And how could he resist a picnic outdoors with all kinds of food?

My head was spinning as I wandered over to the other kids. They were lining up, getting ready to go on some of the carnival rides.

Bernardo grabbed my arm. "Jordan, let's move, dude," he said. He began pulling me away.

"Hey—where are we going?" I cried. "Where are you taking me?"

"You'll see," Bernardo replied, grinning.

And that's how I ended up in the Tunnel of Fear.

I had no choice. Bernardo wouldn't let go of me. Was this the *last* place on earth I wanted to be? Three guesses.

But here I was, alone in the moving car. Bernardo sat in the car ahead of me. And I gripped the sides of the car and tried to ignore the horrible screams and cruel laughter and skeletons and zombies that popped out at me every few feet.

When the car stuttered and stalled, I cried out, "I don't believe it." Not again! But yes, the car had stopped in total darkness, and the evil laughter stopped with it.

A cold shudder ran down my back. And I remembered how terrifying it had been the last time I was on this awful ride.

But this time, the lights came on immediately. All the lights flashed on overhead, and I blinked in the sudden brightness.

And when I could finally focus my eyes, I let

out a scream that echoed off the tunnel walls. I screamed because I was staring at *myself.*

Yes. It was me. Climbing beside me into the car. Except I knew who it was. I knew it was Robby. This time, he had turned himself into an exact copy of ME.

"You—you can't do this!" I cried.

"Hi, Jordan. It's me—Jordan," he said. A grin spread over his face—MY grin.

"No. You can't. You can't—" I stammered.

"Sure I can," he said.

I gasped, hearing my own voice come out of him.

"I'm going to take over your life, Jordan," he continued. "I'm going to live in your house, and stay in your room—and *eat all your food!*"

"And—and what am *I* supposed to do?" I cried.

He lowered his voice to a cold whisper. "Go away. Go away, Jordan. Take a long trip somewhere. You're no longer needed here."

"No. You can't do this! You *can't!*" I cried.

He gave me a hard shove. He was trying to shove me out of the car.

Panic choked my throat. What could I do?

Then I saw Mr. Ferber and his two workers. I saw them running toward us with the net raised.

"Catch him! Catch him! Don't let him get away!" I choked out.

Then I screamed as the net came down.

33

Wouldn't you know it?

Ferber captured the wrong Jordan.

I screamed and yelled and begged. I tried to let him know he had the wrong Jordan. But, of course, he didn't believe me.

Would you?

And that's why I'm sitting in this cage at the back of the carnival. People are coming by, reading the sign that says PLEASE DO NOT FEED THE WEIRDO. They're staring at me like I'm some kind of freak.

I'm not real worried. I know they'll discover their mistake soon. Then they'll come and let me out.

But in the meantime, I'm really hungry.

Doesn't anyone have any food they could share with me?

"Please, everyone—just ignore the sign. Can anyone share a little food? I'm really starving."

ESCAPE FROM SHUDDER MANSION

Here's a sneak peek!

1

Every time I see the huge, old mansion, my mouth goes dry, and I feel a chill tighten the back of my neck. When you step into the yard, you can feel the temperature drop at least ten degrees.

I guess that's because the ancient trees are so tall, they block out most of the sunlight. But I think the cold is coming from the house, seeping out through the cracked windows and crooked doors.

With its black slate roof and high stone towers, the house rises above the treetops and casts a deep shadow, no matter the time of day.

The house is nearly hidden by the trees. You have to step far into the yard until its dark walls and even blacker windows come into view.

By that time, it's *too late*. Too late to escape its ghostly coldness . . . too late to escape the evil as it curls around you and freezes you in its icy grip.

Okay, okay.

I know I got a little carried away there. You don't know me yet. If you knew me, you would know that sometimes I get excited and go a little overboard.

I am Riley Shiner. I'm twelve. My twin sister, Scarlet, knows me best. Scarlet says I'm just like her guitar. Sometimes the strings get wound too tight and make a shrill sound.

She says I'm just like those strings. Wound too tight.

LOL, right? I can't argue with Scarlet. And I can't get angry at her because she makes me laugh. Scarlet is funny.

People expect a lot from you when you're twins. For one thing, they expect you to look alike. Well . . . Scarlet and I don't.

She is tall and thin and has wavy red hair and blue eyes. I'm about three inches shorter and a little chubby, and my hair and eyes are dark brown.

When people meet us for the first time, they don't think we're twins. They don't even think we're brother and sister! "Actually, we're *identical* twins," Scarlet tells people. That always cracks us both up. Most people just get confused.

"You have to listen to me, Riley," Scarlet says. "Because I'm twelve minutes older than you."

I don't know if she means that or not. Does she

really think she can boss me around because she's the big sister?

So, it was after school and she was leading the way through the trees in back of Shudder Mansion. Yes. Shudder Mansion. The name of the house says it all. It was maybe the *last place* I wanted to be.

I stepped in front of her to block her path. "Scarlet, why do we have to go this way? You know the stories about this place."

"It's a shortcut," she said.

"And we're in a hurry because . . . ?"

"I'm late for my Wednesday guitar lesson," she said.

"But today is Thursday!" I protested.

"That means I'm *really* late!"

I told you. She's funny.

She pushed me out of her way and started walking a zigzag path through the trees. I gazed at the back of the house. The stone walls were cracked—long cracks that looked like lightning bolts. Two back windows were boarded up, the glass missing.

I felt another chill.

"Scarlet, this isn't going to save us any time," I said.

"Not if you keep stopping," she said. She narrowed her blue eyes at me. "You don't really believe the stories about this mansion—do you?"

"Maybe," I said. The word came out in a

squeak. "Look at this place," I said, motioning with one hand. "It *has* to be evil."

She shook her head. "Seriously. You have got to stop playing that video game."

You have to understand. Shudder Mansion is so scary and so famous, there is an awesome, bestselling video game about it. The game is called *Escape from Shudder Mansion*. And to tell the truth, I'm kind of obsessed with it.

I mean, how many games take place right in your neighborhood? The game starts two blocks from my house!

I'd played it so much, I knew every room, every twist and turn of the dark halls. It's about these evil spirits that are trapped in the house. They want revenge for their fate on anyone who ventures into the house.

As you play, you accumulate weapons. The idea is you have to destroy each evil spirit before it can kill you—or you will become one of them, trapped in Shudder Mansion forever.

I've made it to the Fourth Level. It wasn't easy. I had a lot of scary moments and close calls and I died a lot.

Scarlet keeps telling me it's just a game. But . . . where did the idea for the game come from? It came from the real Shudder Mansion. And what if the game makers were telling the truth? What if they didn't make the story up?

A lot of horror movies are based on true stories, right?

So I think you can see why I didn't want to take a shortcut through the back lawn. Even if Scarlet was late for her guitar lesson.

"Come on, Riley. Hurry," she said. "Stop looking at the house."

Standing in a small clearing of trees, I couldn't take my eyes off it. I squinted into the shadowy, flickering light—and thought I saw something. Something like smoke, narrow and black. I watched it float out of one of the broken windows.

I gasped. "Scarlet—look—"

But she was far ahead of me, making her way through the trees.

Unable to breathe, or move, I watched the black shadow grow larger as it whirled away from the mansion. Blacker than the shadows, like a cloud of ink, it curled low to the ground, taking the shape of a snake, slithering, folding in on itself, raising a fanged, triangle-shaped head.

It's coming for me, I realized.

And then I remembered this black snaky creature—from the video game!

I've seen it. I've seen it—and I've never defeated it.

Silently, it slid and curled over the grass, in a straight line now, a straight line toward me. This black serpent shadow.

My whole body went cold. As it slithered closer, I could feel its evil washing around me.

I could feel it. I could feel it. The whole yard turning dark now.

I opened my mouth in a scream—spun around—and started to run.

I stumbled over a clump of tall weeds. My back-pack flew over my head as I tumbled to the ground. I landed hard. The breath shot out of me with a loud *whoosh*, and pain spread over my chest.

I wanted to scramble to my feet, but I couldn't breathe. I rolled onto my back, choking, gasping for air.

I raised my head and saw the black shadow coming closer. I watched it rise up like a tall ocean wave. It spread out and rose higher, higher. Then it swept over me.

I lay there helpless, still unable to breathe, smothered in its coldness now, covered in black-ness. And inside the shadow, deep inside, I saw the glow, the blazing glow of red eyes.

Red eyes flaming inside a monstrous face, a face twisted and distorted, with lips like fat worms, lips that opened to reveal two sets of pointed gray teeth.

I stared helplessly at the glowing red eyes as the shadow creature spread its blackness over me. I shivered and shook. I struggled to toss it off.

But it clung to me. Wrapped itself tightly around my shoulders. And started to shake me hard.

It shook me. Shook me so hard my teeth rattled. I struggled to see it in the total darkness.

And then the shadow lifted. I blinked as the trees above me came into focus. Rays of yellow sunlight flashed and flickered in the leaves.

I gazed up. It was Scarlet, shaking me by the shoulders—not the monster inside the black cloud. She had both hands on my shoulders. She was on her knees, leaning over me, shaking me.

Where was the evil shadow?

Scarlet finally let go and climbed to her feet. "What's wrong, Riley?" she demanded. "Why are you on the ground?"

I raised my head. "A shadow—" I murmured.

"Get up. What are you doing down there?" She lowered a hand to pull me to my feet.

But I didn't take her hand. Instead, I stared at the creature beside me in the grass. A cat. A green-eyed black cat.

"Whoa!" I uttered a cry and jumped up.

Scarlet laughed. "Is that what scared you? A black cat?"

"N-no," I stammered.

The cat tilted its head to one side and stared up at me without blinking.

It's not a cat, Scarlet, I thought, my heart pounding. *It's some kind of shadow creature from the house. I didn't imagine it. This is not really a cat.*

Scarlet tugged my T-shirt sleeve. "Let's go. Don't you know you can't win a staring contest with a cat?"

Before I could move, the cat hissed at me and swiped a paw in the air.

I jumped back.

My sister laughed. "That cat doesn't like you."

"I don't like it, either," I whispered. I squinted down at it and tried to read its eyes. I knew I was right about it.

"Get over it," Scarlet said. "You can't be afraid of a black cat, Riley. Look how tame and sweet it is."

I watched it spin away from me, raising its tail high behind it. The cat loped off through the tall weeds, then silently padded over the grass toward the mansion.

And as it ran, it appeared to dissolve. It just melted away. Poof. It became a blob of smoke again. When it neared the mansion, floating over the lawn, it faded into a flickering shadow.

Then I gasped as the shadow exploded. It burst apart, into a million pieces. Like dandelion seeds when you blow on them. I stood frozen, watching the tiny bits of shadow blow apart, float high over the grass, and disappear.

"Did you see that, Scarlet?" I screamed. "Did you see that?"

She was bent over, picking my backpack up from where I'd dropped it. "See *what*, Riley?"

"The cat—it—it—" I sputtered.

"It ran away. So what?"

"No. You don't understand. The cat—" I stopped with my mouth hanging open. I squinted into the shadowy light to the low stone wall that ran along the back of the yard.

Something moved along the wall.

There was someone there. A girl. Standing very still, under a tree that overhung the wall.

I squinted harder. "Who is *that*?"

About the Author

R.L. Stine's books are read all over the world. So far, his books have sold more than 300 million copies, making him one of the most popular children's authors in history. Besides Goosebumps, R.L. Stine has written the teen series Fear Street and the funny series Rotten School, as well as the Mostly Ghostly series, The Nightmare Room series, and the two-book thriller *Dangerous Girls*. R.L. Stine lives in New York with his wife, Jane, and Minnie, his King Charles spaniel. You can learn more about him at www.RLStine.com.

www.scholastic.com/goosebumps